P9-BII-770

His son.

He rolled the weight of those two words around in his mind, feeling them, savoring them. He'd actually felt like a father tonight. Or at least, the way he imagined being a father would feel.

And he had Melanie to thank.

In Cord's entire life, no one had believed he was worth a damn. No one except Mel. And here she was believing again, after all that had happened, after all he'd done.

He wanted to lie down on the bed next to her and let the sway of the boat beneath them lull him into a dreamworld from which he never had to wake.

Too bad that wasn't possible.

7-10-06

ANN VOSS PETERSON

VOW TO PROTECT

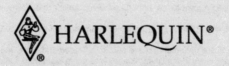

HARLEQUIN®

TORONTO • NEW YORK • LONDON
AMSTERDAM • PARIS • SYDNEY • HAMBURG
STOCKHOLM • ATHENS • TOKYO • MILAN • MADRID
PRAGUE • WARSAW • BUDAPEST • AUCKLAND

If you purchased this book without a cover you should be aware that this book is stolen property. It was reported as "unsold and destroyed" to the publisher, and neither the author nor the publisher has received any payment for this "stripped book."

To John, who holds my hand
while we watch our sons sleep.
And special thanks to the Middleton Police Department
for filling my notebook with answers
to my many questions.

ISBN-13: 978-0-373-22937-6
ISBN-10:   0-373-22937-2

VOW TO PROTECT

Copyright: © 2006 by Ann Voss Peterson

All rights reserved. Except for use in any review, the reproduction or utilization of this work in whole or in part in any form by any electronic, mechanical or other means, now known or hereafter invented, including xerography, photocopying and recording, or in any information storage or retrieval system, is forbidden without the written permission of the publisher, Harlequin Enterprises Limited, 225 Duncan Mill Road, Don Mills, Ontario, Canada M3B 3K9.

All characters in this book have no existence outside the imagination of the author and have no relation whatsoever to anyone bearing the same name or names. They are not even distantly inspired by any individual known or unknown to the author, and all incidents are pure invention.

This edition published by arrangement with Harlequin Books S.A.

® and TM are trademarks of the publisher. Trademarks indicated with ® are registered in the United States Patent and Trademark Office, the Canadian Trade Marks Office and in other countries.

www.eHarlequin.com

Printed in U.S.A.

ABOUT THE AUTHOR

Ever since she was a little girl making her own books out of construction paper, Ann Voss Peterson wanted to write. So when it came time to choose a major at the University of Wisconsin, creative writing was her only choice. Of course, writing wasn't a *practical* choice—one needs to earn a living. So Ann found jobs ranging from proofreading legal transcripts, to working with quarter horses, to washing windows. But no matter how she earned her paycheck, she continued to write the type of stories that captured her heart and imagination—romantic suspense. Ann lives near Madison, Wisconsin, with her husband, her two young sons, her border collie and her quarter horse mare. Ann loves to hear from readers. E-mail her at ann@annvosspeterson.com or visit her Web site at annvosspeterson.com.

Books by Ann Voss Peterson

*Wedding Mission

CAST OF CHARACTERS

Cordell "Cord" Turner—An ex-convict, Cord doesn't believe he has much to offer. But when his father, serial killer Dryden Kane, threatens the woman he loved and lost as a teen, Cord can't help making a vow to protect her...and the son he never knew he had.

Melanie Frist—When Cord was imprisoned for killing another teen in a gang fight, Melanie cut off all contact, even when she learned she was pregnant with his child. Now she will do anything to protect her son, from Dryden Kane...and from following in Cord's footsteps.

Dryden Kane—When a horrible accident sets the notorious serial killer free, he takes stock of what is most important. And to him, the most important thing in the world is family. Right up there with manipulation, domination and control.

Ethan Frist—Like any nine-year-old boy, Ethan needs a dad.

Reporter Aidan Powell—He seems to have a source on the inside. Who is it?

Detective Reed McCaskey—He is determined to bring Dryden Kane down. Once and for all.

Detective Nikki Valducci—As ambitious as she is beautiful, she is determined to build her career on the capture of Dryden Kane.

Detective Stan Perreth—Someone is in the disagreeable detective's sights. Dryden Kane? Or Reed McCaskey?

Officer Herns—He believes people who mess with serial killers deserve what they get.

Meredith Unger—The ace attorney wanted Kane as a client to share in his notoriety. With his escape, is the exposure getting too hot?

Chapter One

Corrections Officer Dale Swiggum would have to tell his grandkids about this one.

Of course, it might help to actually have kids. Hell, it might help to have a regular girlfriend. But with this story in his arsenal, he was sure to impress that sexy little brunette who manned the checkout at the Piggly Wiggly.

He was going to be transferring Dryden Kane down to the county lockup to stand trial.

He leaned back in the driver's seat and smiled. When he'd been notified of the transport just an hour ago, he knew the convict he was hauling had to be important. Most convicts were transported by bus in broad daylight when they had a court date. When an assignment came down in the middle of the night, it had to be something big. But Dryden Kane? The most notorious Wisconsin serial killer since Jeffrey Dahmer? That was bigger than even Dale could dream.

He peered out the bug-spattered windshield of the state van as the giant steel door slid open and four correctional officers led Kane into the underground garage. The killer looked small in his baggy, dayglow-orange jumpsuit. He did the prisoner shuffle, his legs shackled, hands cuffed and locked to a waist chain.

If Dale met him walking down the street, he'd never guess this average-size, good-looking guy with silver hair was a monster who had killed at least a dozen women. Hunted them like deer. And spread them out for the world to find.

Dale would have a story to tell, all right. He wouldn't have to *pretend* he was "about something" as the cons liked to say. He *was* about something.

The correctional officers led the shackled killer into the back of the van. After securing Kane to the bench, two officers climbed into the cage with him. The third climbed up front with Dale, and the fourth joined the chase car.

Dale glanced at the officer beside him. Jerry Brunner was a brute with biceps and a bad attitude almost as big as a con's. He gripped his shotgun like he meant to use it. He likely did.

Good thing Jerry was on Dale's side.

The order to move out came over the radio. Excitement trilled through Dale like he was a boy dumping candy from his stocking on Christmas morning. He shifted the van into gear and fell in behind the unmarked car leading the low-key parade. The overhead door rose in front of them, and the three-vehicle caravan rolled out into the humid Wisconsin night.

The tires hummed along the highway, the sound buzzing in Dale's ears like the adrenaline buzzing in his veins. The county jail and courthouse was only ten minutes away from the Banesbridge Prison, not much of a drive, but he'd soak up the feeling while it lasted. He glanced at Jerry. "How do you think we got picked for this?"

Jerry shrugged. The behemoth never had much to say. He probably had the IQ of that shotgun he was carrying.

The truck started over a low bridge crossing the Wisconsin River. The sound of the tires echoed hollow over the water below. It had been a rainy June, especially up north, and the river swelled high on its banks, the water deep and black as a hole.

Across the narrow span, a pickup's headlights shone high and bright.

Dale squinted and averted his eyes to the white line on the outer edge of the bridge.

"Damn drunk," Jerry said.

The lights bucked and swerved. His radio

crackled to life as the lead car reported the drunk to the county sheriff.

The truck grew closer. It swerved again. Suddenly the glare headed right for the lead car.

Dale stomped the brake. The van skidded.

Ahead, a screech and sickening crunch shook the air.

The cage van veered sideways, rushing up on the wreck in front of them. Dale stomped the brake. The van was too heavy and moving too fast. He wasn't going to be able to stop.

They hit with a wallop. The back of the van skidded around, through the guardrail. Another slam hit from behind, the chase car. The van hurtled over the edge of the bridge.

They hit the black water with a smack. The impact hurled Dale against his seat belt, whipping his neck back and then forward. His forehead slammed the steering wheel.

Pain split his skull. Fog fluttered around him. He struggled to clear his mind, to focus. Voices erupted from the cage. Next to him, Jerry slumped in his seat, something dark glistening on the side of his head. Light from the shore fractured and prismed through the shattered passenger window.

Dale struggled to clear his vision. He forced his mind to focus. They needed help. The radio. He grabbed the radio.

Screams erupted from the cage in the back of the van. "Open the cage! Open the damn cage or we're all going to drown!"

More shouting. The jangle of keys. A gunshot split the air. Then another.

Dale ducked in his seat. He grabbed for the rifle clutched in Jerry's still hands. His head ached so hard, he could hardly cut through the pain to think.

Had one of the C.O.s shot Kane? Or was Kane the one with the gun?

The van felt like it was moving. Drifting. Riding the river. Dale looked up, trying to get a view of the cage in the rearview mirror. The bridge abutment loomed outside the windshield. Concrete scraped along steel. Black water leaked into the van, covering his shoes, inching to his knees. The van's nose dipped low.

They were going down.

He tried to keep the panic from breaking over him like the cold sweat dampening his uniform. He couldn't hear anything from the back. Not another shot. Not the jangle of shackles. Leading with the shotgun, he looked over the seat.

The back of the cage hung open. The dark shadow of a single man slumped on the floor. And judging from his size and the deep-blue color of his uniform, it wasn't Kane.

The killer was gone.

Chapter Two

Cord Turner didn't get invitations. Not to parties. Not to bank credit. Not to anything. Fine with him. He didn't expect to be invited to anything. Hell, he probably wouldn't go if he was. So when he plucked the square white envelope from his afternoon mail and pulled out an invitation to a wedding reception, he had damn good reason to be confused.

Questions buzzed in his mind and drowned out the music playing over his tinny kitchen radio. He stared at the thick white card in his hands, his blunt fingernails coarse and stained against the delicate white embossing. He didn't know anyone who was getting married. Certainly not anyone who would invite him. Hell, he didn't know anyone at all—at least not anyone *worth* knowing—and he'd like to keep it that way.

He opened the card.

Your presence is requested at a reception celebrating the recent marriages of Sylvie and Bryce Walker and Diana and Reed McCaskey. Black tie required.

He moved his eyes to the bottom of the card. There was no signature, no name identifying the party's host, simply a single line.

"The father of the brides."

Cord let the card fall from his hands. During his eight years in prison, Cord had only met a handful of men whose evil radiated in the air around them like heat from a blast furnace. And although he'd never met Dryden Kane, he'd known the killer was such a man the first time he'd seen a picture of Kane's dead ice-blue eyes.

Ice-blue eyes Cord had inherited.

No doubt Cord's half sisters Sylvie and Diana had nothing to do with planning this party. They would want even less to do with their father than they would want with Cord.

He picked up the card and thick, foiled envelope. He needed to get rid of the damn thing. Diana's cop husband already suspected him of scheming with Kane based on nothing but the fact that the killer's blood was flowing in his veins. One whiff of this invitation and Cord's parole officer would give him a violation so fast he'd be back in the system before the evening news.

About to stuff the card into the envelope and crumple the whole thing into a ball, he noticed a slip of paper still tucked inside. He flipped the envelope upside down. The paper dropped to the counter. A severe black scrawl marred white vellum.

"Melanie Frist will be your date. I'll give her a personal invitation."

The name hit Cord like a kick to the gut. His pulse throbbed in his ears, overwhelming the radio commercials leading to the three-o'clock news.

How did Kane know about his past with Mel? And since the killer was in prison, what did he mean by a "personal invitation"?

Cord eyed his cordless phone lying among his other mail on the kitchen counter. She wouldn't want to talk to him. She hadn't visited him in jail, hadn't attended his sentencing, hadn't visited him in the more than eight years he'd spent behind bars. And he would bet she hadn't tried to look him up in the two years since he'd been paroled. She wasn't going to change her mind about seeing him now.

But did that matter in light of a threat from a serial killer?

He ran his gaze back over the scrawled note.

He'd seen evil. He'd smelled it. He'd lived it. And one of the first things he'd learned in the joint was you never turned your back on it.

He picked up the telephone and punched in the four numbers before setting it back down. If Mel had caller ID, he doubted she would pick up. Not if she saw his name on the screen. He'd have to drive to her house. To face her.

Fishing his truck keys from his pocket, he tried to ignore the jittery feeling that seized him low in his stomach. He reached to switch off the radio. The urgent tone of the announcer's voice stopped him cold.

"The Banes County Sheriff's Department has issued a warning to all residents in southern Wisconsin after an accident early this morning claimed the lives of an unidentified man and four officers from the Banesbridge Correctional Facility and hospitalized one additional officer. The accident involved a convoy that was transporting incarcerated serial killer Dryden Kane from the prison to the Banes County jail to be arraigned on new charges stemming from the copycat-killer investigation. The sheriff's office is dragging the Wisconsin River bed, but the serial killer's body has not yet been found. If alive, Dryden Kane is considered armed and extremely…"

Cord didn't wait for the rest. He raced for the door, his truck keys' sharp edges digging into his palm.

WHEN MELANIE STEPPED out the door of her house shortly after arriving home, the main thing on her mind was retrieving the day's collection of mail-order catalogs, credit card offers and bills from the box.

All thoughts of mail vanished the moment she saw Cord.

He slammed the door of a small gray pickup and strode up the sidewalk. He'd been a boy of eighteen when she'd last seen him. Now he was a man. The baby fat was gone from his face, replaced by sharp angles and hard planes. Tattoos covered thick, strong arms that strained the sleeves of his T-shirt. Powerful thighs filled out faded jeans.

A wave of heat washed over her, followed by panic. "Why are you here?"

He closed the gap between them. Swirling with light blue the color of a winter sky, his eyes drilled into her. Eyes that hadn't changed. Not one bit. "We have to talk."

Alarm writhed inside her. She couldn't stand here and talk. What did he expect to chat about? How he'd nearly ruined her life? How he'd broken her heart? "No. No we don't."

"Mel, please. I know it's a shock to see me. I wouldn't have come if I didn't have a damn good reason."

She crossed her arms over her chest and forced herself to stand her ground. If only she could hop in her car, drive away and avoid this entire reunion. But she couldn't. Ethan would be getting off the bus any minute.

Ethan.

Her mind stuttered.

This was worse than an uncomfortable re-union. Worse than reliving a broken heart and shattered dreams. Much worse. This was Ethan's future in jeopardy.

She glanced down the street. A red convertible streaked down the pavement toward them, moving too fast in the residential neighborhood. A squatty white mail truck stopped at the opposite curb. No sign of a bus.

She had time.

She swung her focus back to Cord. If he was still anything like the boy she'd once loved, he wouldn't leave until he'd said his piece. Her best bet would be to hear him out then cut him off. "Why are you here?"

He cleared his throat as if preparing to launch into a rehearsed speech. "You have to get out of here."

She didn't know what she'd expected him to say, but it wasn't this. "Why?"

"A man is after you. A bad man. You understand what I'm saying?"

She didn't have a clue. "Who's after me?"

"Dryden Kane."

She couldn't have heard him right. "The serial killer?"

"He escaped this morning."

"I heard." In the world of serial killers, Dryden Kane was as infamous in Wisconsin history as Dahmer and Gein. But while Kane was a very dangerous man, especially to women, there were thousands of women in southern Wisconsin. "Why do you think he's after me?"

"Because he told me."

Now he was really freaking her out. "What are you up to, Cord? Why are you saying this?"

He raked a hand across short sandy-brown hair. "I don't know how the hell to explain. I can still hardly believe it myself."

She fought the urge to grab him, to shake him. "Just say it."

"Dryden Kane is my father."

"Your father?" She let her arms fall limp to her sides. It couldn't be true. Could it? "You always told me you didn't know who your father was."

"I didn't. Not until about two months ago."

"And it's Dryden Kane? You're sure?"

"Have you seen a picture of Kane recently? I look just like him."

"That doesn't mean—"

"Yes, it does. I had a DNA test done after I found out."

She felt sick to her stomach.

"You have to come with me. Kane might be on his way right now. Understand what I'm saying?"

"I'm not going anywhere."

"Mel, you have to."

"I want you off my property."

"You're not listening."

"I've heard enough." She needed Cord gone. Right now.

"You have to get out of here."

She intended to. Just not with him. When Ethan got home, she'd whisk her son off to a safe place and hold him tight to her heart. Whether Ethan thought he was too old for hugs or not.

"Kane is dangerous."

"Don't you think I know that?" Her stomach balled into a hard knot. She'd struggled so hard. To lift herself out of the violent world she'd grown up in. To give Ethan a real future. And now this. "How dare you bring this stuff back into my life? How dare you bring Dryden Kane down on my head?"

"I'm sorry, Mel. I'm so sorry. But right now you have to get out of here. You have to come with me." He reached out, trying to grasp her arm.

She yanked it away. "If you don't leave, I'm calling the police."

"Call them."

"What?"

"Call the cops. Go with them. I don't care. You just have to get out of here before Kane shows up."

"Okay. I'll call them. Now go."

"I'll stay until they get here."

"Not necessary." She gave the traffic a quick glance. Something caught her eye beyond the building afternoon glut of panel vans and sports cars. A flash of yellow turning off a side street.

"He might be watching us right now."

"I don't want your help. You'll only make things worse."

"Listen, I've seen what guys like this can do, what they enjoy doing. It ain't nothing nice."

"Leave me alone."

"I'm not leaving until I know you'll be safe."

She glanced down the street again. Behind a blue minivan and a white sedan, the bright yellow school bus barreled toward them.

"What are you looking for?"

A thick ache lodged in her throat. "Nothing. Nothing at all." The school bus rumbled up the street, desperation drilling deeper into her bones the closer it came.

Chapter Three

Lines dug into Mel's smooth forehead as the school bus's brakes squealed to a stop at the bottom of her driveway.

Cord had expected her to be upset to see him. He'd expected her to be scared. He hadn't expected her to be more nervous about a damn yellow bus than she was about Dryden Kane.

The red stop sign swung out from the driver's side, and the door opened. A skinny boy shouldered a backpack far too big for him and clomped down the bus steps. He hopped onto the pavement and started up the drive's slope. Looking up at Melanie, he offered her a little smile, a playful light twinkling in his ice-blue eyes.

Eyes identical to Cord's.

Identical to Dryden Kane's.

Cord jerked back as if he'd been kicked in the

grill. He fought to regain breath, to regain thought. "How old is he?"

Melanie tensed beside him, but she didn't answer.

"How old is he, Mel?"

"Ten."

Ten years old. He didn't have to ask if the boy was his son. He knew. Down to the marrow of his bones, he knew.

"I found out the day you killed Snake."

And she hadn't told him. She hadn't come to see him in jail. She hadn't come to his trial. She hadn't even answered his phone calls.

The boy ambled up the driveway toward them. Lanky and skinny, he moved as if he was growing too fast for his coordination to catch up. Eight more years, and he'd be eighteen. Legally a man. The age Cord was when the kid had been conceived. When Cord had been thrown in prison.

He tried to speak, to move, to do anything that didn't involve standing and staring, but he came up empty.

"I had to get him away from the neighborhood. I didn't want him to live that life, to spend his Sundays in a prison visiting room like I did. I didn't want him to follow that path. I—"

He held up a hand to cut her off. She didn't have to explain. "You were right not to tell me. You were right to give him a better life." The life they'd planned together before he was arrested. The life Melanie had dreamed for them both.

Her gaze burned hot on the side of his face. "Don't say anything. *Please.* He doesn't know you're his father. I told him his father died."

Cord *had* died in prison. He'd died every day since he'd killed Snake. "He won't learn it from me."

The boy crested the drive and started up the walk. The afternoon sun slanted down on his face and illuminated the dusting of freckles sprinkling the bridge of his nose, almost invisible under the remnants of his summer tan. His sandy-brown hair fell low on his forehead, straight as straw, refusing to cooperate with its new back-to-school cut. And though not large, his ears perked out from the sides of his head as if on alert.

It was like staring at a photo of himself as a child.

Numbness gave way to heat swirling in his head and burning down the back of his neck. An empty feeling hollowed out under his rib cage.

"Hey, Mom." The kid gave Melanie another small smile, as if the two of them shared a funny secret, a special joke. Then he looked at Cord, focusing on the tattoos ringing Cord's biceps and stretching down his arms. Barbed wire. A headless snake. The writhing forms of dragons. The lines thick and chunky, more symbols than art.

What was the kid seeing? Did he notice the resemblance? The eyes they shared? The rectangular chin? Or was he just seeing the ex-con? The criminal? The man with no future?

"Ethan, this is Cord."

Ethan. His son was named Ethan.

The boy nodded. "Hi."

Cord willed his voice to function. "Hi."

"Cord was just leaving. And so are we."

He managed to tear his eyes away from Ethan and direct them to Mel. The void in his gut seemed to widen. "I'll follow you to the police station. Make sure you get there safely."

She looked away. "Do what you want."

"You're a cop?" Ethan's eyebrows dipped low over his eyes.

"No."

"He's someone I knew a long time ago. That's all."

Cord nodded. That *was* all. He'd killed the rest as surely as he'd killed Snake. As he'd killed his own future.

Tires screeched, the sound echoing from the street.

Cord spun around just as a police cruiser whipped into the driveway. Three cars followed. Jolting to angled stops, the cops hunkered down behind the open driver's doors, guns drawn.

"Police!" a voice barked, deep and threatening. "Hands up! As high as you can reach! Now!"

Cord's mouth went dry. He raised his hands, stretching as high as he could. The familiar mix of adrenaline and humiliation tightened his throat and coated his tongue.

Movement shifted and rustled from around the house and yard. Cops fanned out from their cars, semiautos and rifles leveled on him, Kevlar vests dark and oppressive in the early-September heat.

A cop approached Melanie and Ethan. In less than a second, he whisked them away from Cord and out of the line of fire.

At least they wouldn't be hurt. Cord could focus on that.

"Keep your hands above your head and slowly turn around."

Hands high, Cord pivoted. He turned slowly, allowing them to see he had no bulges of weapons in the waistband of his jeans, no reason to believe he was dangerous. As much as he wanted to ask why they were doing this, he kept his mouth shut. He knew how cops thought. He was an ex-con. He had nothing coming. Not even an explanation. And he sure as hell wasn't going to egg them on by demanding one.

"Keep turning."

He turned another 180, until he was facing back toward Melanie.

She crossed her arms around Ethan's chest and

held him tight, protecting him. The boy watched with wide eyes, as if he'd never seen a scene quite like this. No doubt he never had. It sure as hell wasn't a scene from his world.

It was a scene from Cord's.

"Put your hands on the top of your head," the cop ordered.

Cord did as he was told, lacing his fingers together the way he'd been taught.

"Down on your knees. Take it slow."

Cord lowered himself. One knee and then the other hit the pavement. He didn't have to wonder how Ethan saw him now. He just hoped it wouldn't take the kid long to forget him.

"Down on your belly. Arms away from your body. Palms facing up. Cross your ankles."

Cord had done this maneuver enough while in prison to perform it in his sleep. He flattened himself to the ground and crossed his legs. Cheek pressed against the hot driveway, he moved his arms wide, palms up.

Boots scuffed the concrete around him. A hand grabbed his arm and bent it behind his back. A steel handcuff closed around his wrist. The cop grabbed his other arm, cuffing it to the first. The inflexible bands of steel bit into his wrists, bruising his flesh. Hands patted his sides and legs. Once satisfied he was clean, the cop rolled him to his side. "Rise to your knees."

Cord struggled into a kneeling position at the cop's feet.

"Cross your ankles."

Cord did what he was told. Why didn't they take Melanie and Ethan away? Why didn't they take them into the house where they didn't have to watch, where the fact of what he was wasn't in their faces? "What is this about?"

"Shut up."

He should have known better than to ask. He had nothing coming. The old prison saying was just as true on this side of the razor wire.

A dark green sedan crept up the drive and stopped behind the cruisers. The door opened and a dark-haired detective climbed out.

The last time Cord had seen Reed McCaskey, the cop had been marrying Cord's half sister Diana on the shores of Lake Mendota. Cord hadn't been invited, not to the wedding and not to the small reception held on a boat afterward, but he'd stood in the shadow of the park shelter anyway and watched, though to this day, he didn't really understand why.

McCaskey made his way through the parked cruisers and stopped behind the cop who'd been shouting the orders. "This isn't Kane."

The cop gave him a frown. "You sure?"

"Yes. But bring him to the downtown district office. We need to have a talk with him anyway."

The patrol cop nodded. "Parole violation?"

"Possibly. And helping his father escape."

Melanie didn't move. In her embrace, Ethan scuffed the rubber sole of his shoe against the pavement. As if sensing Cord's gaze, the boy raised his eyes.

Then looked away.

MELANIE HELD ON to Ethan's shoulders, a tremor seizing her and questions spinning through her mind. Just an hour ago she'd had her life just the way she'd wanted. A great job at the lab. A secure home for her son. A sane and safe neighborhood in which he could grow up and thrive.

And then Cord had walked back into her life and brought all her worst nightmares with him.

She looked down at the top of her son's head. Ethan had no idea Cord was his father, but that didn't prevent him from watching Cord's arrest with wide eyes, soaking in every detail. She had to get him out of here. She'd spent her life making sure he didn't have to witness this kind of thing, that he didn't have to grow up in the world she did. She turned to the police officer who had shunted them out of the line of fire.

"Can I take my son inside?"

"In just a moment, ma'am. Detective McCaskey will want to talk to you first." He nodded his head in the direction of a tall, dark-haired man wearing a police department polo shirt.

The detective wound his way through officers and cars and stopped in front of her. "Do you know this man?"

"Yes. I mean, I did. A long time ago."

"Was he threatening you?"

"No, of course not."

"You can answer honestly. We can keep you safe from him."

"No, he wasn't threatening. He was warning me."

"Warning you? About what?"

She glanced down at Ethan. "Can we talk about this another time?"

The detective followed her gaze. His eyes narrowed on Ethan. Then, as almost a reflex, he glanced back at Cord. "I think I understand."

A tremor lodged in Melanie's chest. She should have known he'd figure it out. Ethan looked so much like Cord, it was frightening. The resemblance had stolen her breath on more than one occasion. And now, seeing the two of them together, McCaskey would have to be blind not to see that they were father and son.

And that that fact meant Ethan was Dryden Kane's grandson.

The thought squeezed the breath from her lungs. She couldn't accept that Ethan shared that monster's blood. She couldn't even *start* to wrap her mind around it. She could only pray the detective wouldn't comment. "We were just leaving when the police arrived."

"Why don't you pack some things and we'll see what we can do as far as protection is concerned? We can talk more after you're settled."

She nodded. She could do that. She would pack some of their things and take Ethan away.

She forced her feet to move up the sidewalk and steps to the front door of the house. She couldn't stop shuddering. Gritting her teeth, she opened the storm door and held it wide for Ethan and the detective, trying not to look back as the officers escorted Cord into the backseat of one of the police cars.

A sob thickened deep in her throat, but she refused to let it loose. She'd been through bad things in her life, and she'd get through this, too. For Ethan she could get through anything.

Leaving Reed McCaskey in the great room, she steered Ethan through the hall and into his bedroom. She pulled a duffel bag out of his closet and spread it open on his bed. "Pick out some clothes, games and books and stuff, too. Okay?"

"How long are we going to be gone?"

"I don't know, sweetheart. A few days. It shouldn't be any more than that." At least she hoped not. "What do you say we go to a place with a pool? Just you and me? It will be fun. Like a vacation."

"What about school?"

Ethan always pretended he didn't care about school. But she'd always suspected he enjoyed seeing his friends and working on school projects more than he let on. "Tomorrow is Friday. You'll only miss a day. You'll be back in school next week."

"And your work?"

She couldn't imagine her supervisor at the lab would be thrilled with the short notice, but it couldn't be helped. "I could use a day off with my favorite guy." She slipped an arm around him and squeezed him close, bending down to kiss him on the forehead.

"Mo-om." He rolled his eyes.

Her lips relaxed into a smile. That was the Ethan she knew. "Make sure you pack your swimming suit."

"Can we stay up in the Dells? At one of the water parks?"

"Maybe." At least Ethan was focusing on the bright side. She only wished she could do the same. But dread gathered inside her like clouds of an approaching thunderstorm.

A storm she couldn't escape.

CORD LEANED BACK in the hard chair in the interrogation room and glanced up at the camera positioned in the corner. It stared down at him, its lens an accusing eye waiting to capture his confession. The only problem was he had nothing to confess.

The only thing drumming through his mind right now was concern for Melanie and thoughts of the son he never knew he had.

The son he would never know.

The door to the interrogation room burst open, and a sour-looking cop with jowls that drooped like laundry hung to dry stepped into the room. He closed the door behind him and ran his gaze over the tats on Cord's arms. His upper lip curled in disgust.

Cord was used to the contempt of cops. Long before he'd gone to prison, he'd been the wrong kind of kid, not a hardcore gang banger but close enough. At least in most cops' eyes. He returned the cop's glare with a *Murder One* stare of his own.

The cop was the first to break the silence. "Time to talk, dawg."

Cord hadn't been called dawg since he was behind bars. A memory this cop obviously wanted him to relive. "And you are?"

"Detective Stan Perreth." He glanced down at his watch. "You have five minutes to come clean, or I'm calling your parole officer. I hear your friends are throwing a par-tay in your cell and everyone's coming. You understand what I'm saying?"

This guy was a riot. A regular prison jargon stand-up show, albeit a little cleaner than the language flying around the joint. "How about you call my lawyer first?"

"Why? You got something to hide?" Perreth plunked into a chair and leaned close. Table shoved to the side of the room, there was nothing between him and the cop. The odor of cigarette smoke emanating from Perreth's clothing and breath was enough to make Cord crave a rollie of his own, though he'd kicked the habit when he'd been paroled. "It's in your best interest to talk," Perreth said.

Right. "I don't see how it's in my best interest to have anything to do with you."

"You should *want* to talk to me, punk. I can see to it that Melanie Frist and her boy are safe. Or should I say, *your* boy?"

Cord's gut clenched. He wasn't surprised Perreth noticed the resemblance. One look and anyone could guess Ethan was his son. But Cord didn't like the implication that Mel and Ethan's safety hinged on him confessing to something he didn't know about and didn't do. "Is that some kind of threat?"

"I'm just saying if you help me, I'll be more inclined to help you. That's how the world works."

That might be true. But it still didn't tell Cord what he was supposed to be confessing to in order to earn Perreth's favors.

A sharp knock sounded, and the door opened.

Cord never thought he'd be happy to see his brother-in-law. He sure as hell didn't have a stash of good feelings for Reed McCaskey, but after chatting with Perreth, McCaskey seemed like a long-lost friend. At least he didn't think McCaskey would resort to using Mel and Ethan to get what he wanted.

A female detective with the face of a super-model and the edgy stare of a barracuda stepped into the room behind McCaskey. Cord had met her before, on the same day McCaskey and Diana had dropped the news that Kane was his father.

She stood behind McCaskey, letting him take the lead. But she was no shrinking violet. She had more in common with a sleek and beautiful Doberman pinscher with a keen eye for weakness and no qualms about attacking.

McCaskey nodded to Perreth. "We'll take this, Stan."

Perreth shoved his chair back and puffed out his chest. For a moment Cord wondered if he was going to get the chance to watch a cop pissing match, but Perreth turned and stomped from the room without lowering his fly.

McCaskey and Valducci assumed the chairs facing Cord. Plunking a stack of files on the table at his elbow, McCaskey took the lead. "We need to ask you a few questions."

"And here I thought you dragged me in here for a social visit. You know, a little catching up among family."

McCaskey didn't react. Next to him, Nikki Valducci leaned forward, as if she was anticipating the taste of blood and was just waiting for McCaskey's go-ahead to take a piece out of him.

In contrast, McCaskey leaned back in his chair, the picture of calm control. "Where were you last night, Turner?"

"This again?" Cord really had to start documenting his every move. Maybe then his brother-in-law would get off his back. "Why don't you just tell me what you think I did this time so I can get right to denying it?"

"Have you been in contact with Dryden Kane?"

He thought of the invitation and the scrawled note that had sent him racing to protect Melanie. "Are Melanie Frist and her son in a safe place?"

"They're in protective custody."

Cord blew a breath through tense lips.

"Answer the question, Turner. Have you been in contact with Dryden Kane?"

As long as Mel and Ethan were safe, the invi-

tation didn't matter. All admitting to receiving it
would do was give McCaskey an excuse to violate
Cord's parole and send him back to serve the rest
of his fifteen-year term behind bars. "Have I con-
tacted Kane? No."

McCaskey's eyes narrowed to dark slits. "Then
how did you know Melanie Frist and her son were
in danger? Or did you just make that up?"

So much for avoiding a parole violation. "Kane
sent me an invitation for a wedding reception. You
and Diana and Sylvie and her husband are the
guests of honor."

A muscle twitched along McCaskey's jaw. "And
what does Melanie Frist have to do with this?"

"She's supposed to be my date."

"And your son?"

Cord wanted to think that Kane didn't know
about Ethan. But seeing that the killer seemed to
know about everything else, it was probably
wishful thinking. "If you take me back to my apartment, I'll turn it over to you."

"No need. The lieutenant probably secured a
warrant to search your apartment by now."

A search warrant. This had gone farther than
he'd guessed. "What exactly do you suspect me of
doing?"

"I imagine you've heard about this morning's
accident. The one involving your father."

"I heard." Since he'd learned Kane was his father, he'd followed stories of the serial killer in the local news. He'd heard how Kane had controlled another serial killer from his prison cell like a puppet master. He'd heard how, even though locked behind bars, he'd tried to kill his daughter Diana—Cord's half sister and McCaskey's wife. And of course, there was the accident. "It's been all over the news."

Detective Valducci shifted in her chair with the impatience of an attack dog pulling at her chain. "When is the last time you saw Eddie Trauten?"

A wave of heat washed through Cord. He kept his expression carefully frozen.

McCaskey gave his cover-girl partner an approving glance before narrowing his eyes on Cord. "Recognize the name? Or did he go by a nickname at Waupun?"

If he could, he'd pretend he'd never heard of Eddie Trauten. But after sharing a cell with the whiney little skinhead for six years of his sentence, it might be a little hard to pull off the lie. "What the hell does Eddie have to do with this?"

"Your cellie drove the stolen pickup that slammed into the motorcade transferring Kane. His truck went into the water along with the cage van. The Banes County sheriff fished his body out of the water this morning."

"And Kane? Have they found his body yet?"

"You know they haven't."

Somehow he knew McCaskey would say that. This morning just got better with each passing minute. "I don't know where Kane is. I didn't have anything to do with Eddie breaking him out."

McCaskey gave him a humorless smile. "Somehow I'm not inclined to believe you."

"I don't care what you're inclined to do, it's the truth."

"The truth? I'll bet. You ex-cons wouldn't know truth if it bit you." Valducci smiled showing the teeth she'd no doubt like to do a little biting with.

He was over his head. So far over, he was drowning. "I need to talk to my lawyer."

McCaskey offered a casual shrug of one shoulder. "You sure you want to do that?"

"Why? Are you going to give me the same line as the last detective?"

McCaskey raised a brow. "Line?"

"Yeah. The old chestnut about helping you so you'll help me. You know, that if I want Melanie and Ethan Frist protected, I'll have to confess to whatever you want me to confess to?"

"Is that what Perreth said to you?"

"Pretty much."

That muscle started working again. Apparently

there was more bad blood between McCaskey and Perreth than a simple pissing match could explain.

McCaskey leaned forward, elbows on tabletop, fists clasped at chin level. "Melanie Frist and her son are in protective custody, and they're going to stay there. The only skin you have to worry about saving is your own."

"Okay. Then I'd like my lawyer to help me save it."

"Meredith Unger, right?"

He'd told McCaskey and Valducci to call his attorney when the detectives suspected he was the copycat serial killer. "You have her number in one of those files?" He nodded at the stack looming on the table.

McCaskey kept his eyes riveted to Cord's. "There's one thing you might want to be aware of before you have a heart-to-heart with Meredith Unger."

"And what's that?"

"She has a conflict-of-interest problem you might want to consider."

What kind of game was McCaskey trying to play this time? "I'll bite. What's the problem?"

McCaskey's black eyes drilled into him, as if watching for his reaction, eager to see how he'd take the punch line. "Meredith Unger is your father's attorney. She represents Dryden Kane."

Chapter Four

In prison, when an inmate needed a weapon he could make disappear fast, he filled a sock with something heavy, a handful of batteries, a can of beans. One good swing, and the weapon, known as a slock, could level a man. The revelation that Cord was sharing his attorney with Dryden Kane hit him like a slock to the dome.

One corner of McCaskey's lips lifted in something only a hair short of a smile. "You still want to call your lawyer?"

"I'll pass." When he'd seen Kane's reference to Melanie in the note, he'd wondered where the serial killer had learned of their history. And although he couldn't prove anything, he didn't wonder any longer. "You can't think I had anything to do with Kane's escape. I've never met the man."

"But your attorney has."

Cord wiped a hand across his forehead. Sweat

already dampened his cropped hair. A sign of nerves that McCaskey would no doubt interpret as guilt. "I haven't talked to Meredith Unger for ten years."

"There are a lot of coincidences here, Turner. Coincidences I'm having a hard time swallowing. Meredith Unger. Eddie Trauten."

Cord let out a breath. He couldn't deny the apparent connection between him and Kane through his attorney. He couldn't deny his own connection to Eddie Trauten. But maybe he didn't have to. Maybe those connections were the point. "I don't know what you think of me, McCaskey, but I'm not a stupid man."

McCaskey narrowed his eyes. "Go on."

"If I wanted to help someone like Dryden Kane escape from prison, I wouldn't set up my own cellie to do it. The prison yard is a big place. There are a lot of punks I could recruit for the job. Punks that would force you cops to at least break a sweat before you tied them to me."

"I'm listening."

"I don't want Dryden Kane out. The only thing he is to me is a threat. A danger to Melanie. And a danger to my son."

McCaskey watched him with sharp, nearly black eyes. A slow, agonizing minute ticked by before he finally pushed back from the table, the legs of his chair screeching across the linoleum tile. He glanced at Detective Valducci and then back to Cord. "We'll be back." He stood and walked out, Valducci in his wake, letting the door thunk closed behind him.

Cord forced a breath of stale air into his lungs. He was probably over his head on this one. Hell, he'd been over his head since before he was born. Unfortunately, unlike the gang bangers he'd hung out with as a kid and the cons he'd done time with, he was smart enough to recognize the fact that he was drowning in sewage.

Just not smart enough to do anything about it.

The door opened and McCaskey entered alone. "I just heard from the officers searching your apartment."

He let silence lie between them as if waiting for Cord to acknowledge something incriminating they'd found in an effort to explain it away.

Too bad nothing like that existed. "They found the invitation I told you about?"

"They did."

"And the note threatening Melanie Frist?"

"Yes."

"You've looked through my apartment. I've told you everything I know. So am I under arrest?"

"No. You can go."

Cord nodded but he didn't let himself feel relief. Not yet. "Will Melanie and Ethan be protected?"

McCaskey drilled into him with that black gaze. "You have my word."

Cord slumped against the back of his chair. A trickle of sweat ran over his temple and wound around his ear.

McCaskey might have thrown him a life preserver this time, but Cord had the feeling this ordeal was far from over.

CORD STOOD IN THE OPEN DOOR of his apartment and looked at the mess the cops had made of his place. In the joint, the inmates were obsessed with receiving respect. The smallest slight, like one of the dawgs failing to say "what up?" in the yard was an affront to one's manhood. It was times like this that made Cord grateful he didn't have that respect/disrespect hangup. Life as a con and an ex-con was easier once you acknowledged you didn't much respect yourself. At least then it wasn't a bitter pill when others didn't respect you, either.

"Cord Turner?"

He spun around, expecting to see a cop coming back for a second try at strewing his belongings over every inch of floor. Instead a bookish man with a smart-ass smile and wire-rimmed glasses peered at him from the hallway.

"Who the hell are you?" Cord asked.

"Aidan Powell. I'm with the *Capital Times.*"

A reporter. Cord almost groaned out loud. "Why are you here?"

"I've heard from a reliable source that you are the son of Dryden Kane."

Cord felt sick. He knew reporters would eventually unearth that fact. With the building media frenzy over the serial killer, it was inevitable. But he'd hoped it would take longer than this. "Who told you that?"

"Is it true?"

He grabbed the door. "If you insist on answering my question with a question, you can do it through a closed door."

He held up a hand, blocking the door. "Wait."

"You're going to tell me who is spreading this crap?"

"I heard it the same place I heard that Kane also has a grandson. A kid by the name of Ethan Frist."

Cord pushed the door aside. Reaching out, he grabbed the reporter by the shirt. "Where did you hear that?" Heat crept up his neck. Pressure built in his head.

"Does Kane know?"

"Tell me where you heard it." He hadn't even known he had a son until a few hours ago. But a reporter knew? A reporter who would write about it in his rag for Dryden Kane to see. If the monster didn't already know he had a grandson, he would now. Cord gave the guy a shake.

The guy's glasses flew, landing somewhere in the mess strewn over Cord's apartment's floor. His eyes widened, as if he had finally figured out he'd made a mistake. "Hold on."

"I want an answer," Cord demanded.

"Hey, back off." Powell's voice trembled along with his chin. "Everybody knows. Not just me."

"Everybody?"

"The TV news crews have had it for the past half hour. I'm the only one who cared enough to get a confirmation."

A half hour? After Cord had left the police department, he'd had to hop a bus back to Mel's house to get his police-rummaged truck. He'd driven back to his apartment in silence, unable to stomach anything but the worries being broadcast in his own mind.

He tightened his grip on the reporter's shirt, pulling the crisp cotton taut around the little worm's throat. "Did you hear this from the police?"

The reporter's eyes flared.

Bingo.

"Who in the police department gave you the information?"

"I can't tell you that."

"What do you mean you can't tell me?"

"I promised confidentiality. I can't reveal my source."

The guy was scared to the point of pissing his pants. But he chose to protect his source instead of his hide?

Maybe there were idealists left in the world.

Cord released the reporter's shirt, letting him fall back against the door like a sack of laundry. "This isn't just some kid. This is my son. When this hits the airwaves and newspapers, Kane could see it. And if Kane knows about him…" What would the monster do? Cord didn't know. But he sure as hell didn't want to find out.

Aidan Powell picked himself up, straightened his shirt and put on his glasses, then swallowed a few times before meeting Cord's eyes. "That's not all Kane will find out."

"What else?"

"The boy and his mother are staying at a hotel on the west side of town. The TV cameras are over there now."

Staying in a hotel? They weren't merely staying. They were hiding. Hiding from Kane.

And now the serial killer only had to switch on a television set to find out where they were?

As soon as Cord had seen Mel and his son, he knew he had to walk away. He wasn't the kind of man who could be a father. A husband. He couldn't do anything but drag Ethan and Mel down.

But he couldn't walk away—not quite yet.

He might not be able to be part of the family, but neither was he going to sit by and let anyone hurt Ethan or Mel.

Especially not a sick bastard like Dryden Kane.

MELANIE WATCHED ETHAN cross the pool deck and jump cannonball style into the swimming pool. A splash of chlorine-scented water hit the deck in front of her and spattered her legs.

The water felt nice on her skin, cool, and for a moment she wished she were wearing her swimming suit instead of the T-shirt and shorts she'd changed into. The prospect of slipping into the pool, lounging in the hot tub that bubbled under fake palm trees or taking her son's challenge and trying out the slide that curled around the circumference of the indoor water park beckoned on the edge of her mind like a seductive dream.

She rolled her shoulders, trying to relieve the tension aching in her back and arms. Her shirt stuck to her skin, damp with sweat.

If only this really were a vacation, a time to relax with her son instead of just a way to take Ethan's mind off the fact that they were hiding from a serial killer. If only she could dial back time to yesterday, when she and Ethan had a normal life, a good life, filled with neither hair-raising excitement nor tragedy. But if-onlys accomplished nothing. The only real avenue she had was to pray the police would catch Dryden Kane, pray Ethan would never find out the monster was his grandfather, and pray that Cord would stay out of their lives.

She glanced at the police officer standing a few yards from her at the edge of the pool area. Reed McCaskey had assured her that an officer would stay with them until Kane was back behind bars or dead. She should feel safe. Secure. But the vague dread that had started with Cord's appearance at her house continued to build.

She had to get her mind off Kane and off Cord if she was going to hold on to her sanity. She focused on Ethan, on the unbridled fun he and the other children were having. On the far side of the dome, kids crawled over a wrecked pirate ship and zipped down slides springing from the hull.

And beyond them, through the window, something moved. A face peered through the glass.

A gasp caught in Melanie's throat. She stepped closer to get a better look.

A woman stared through the window, scanning the pools and water slides. A bright light turned on behind her, illuminating a van parked along the curb. A van with a cable-news logo emblazoned on the side.

The media?

She glanced back at the warehouse-size room. Ethan perched on top of the longest waterslide, getting into position to take its winding ride into the pool.

Could the media have found out Ethan was Dryden Kane's grandson? Could they be planning to tell the world?

She inhaled a breath of humid, chlorinated air. She couldn't let herself panic. If they knew, there wasn't anything she could do to change it. But she'd be damned if they were going to get footage of her son to go along with the story.

She crossed the pebbled surface of the pool deck to where the cop was keeping watch. "A cable-news crew is outside."

The cop gave her a surprised look and glanced around the pool area. "News crew? Where?"

She pointed at the news crew just as the reporter peered through the window.

He shrugged a shoulder. "They're probably covering some event or something. Don't worry."

"An event? Do you see an event going on in here?"

"You think they're taping you?"

"No, I think they're taping my son."

Pushing out his lower lip, he nodded in a glib way, as if the whole situation was nothing more than an interesting joke.

Didn't he know what kind of monster he was

protecting her and Ethan from? "You aren't taking this seriously."

"I'm taking it plenty seriously. You need to calm down, ma'am."

Calm down? Not until she knew her son was safe. Not until this damn mess was over and her life and Ethan's were back to normal. "Tell them to leave."

"I can't do that."

"Why not? I thought you were here to protect us. If you aren't, I want an officer who will."

"I'll talk to hotel management. They can ask the reporters to leave the property."

"Do that."

He gave her a sideways smirk. He clearly thought she was overreacting.

Fine. Let him think what he wanted. As far as she was concerned, nothing she could do was over-reacting if it meant keeping Ethan safe. She turned back to the pool to find Ethan.

"Where are you going?"

So suddenly he's concerned? She looked back at him. "Why? Are you worried about protecting us now?"

"You don't have reason to be so hostile."

"By disregarding the danger my son is in—danger that news exposure will make worse—you've given me plenty of reason."

The cop's good humor slid from his lips. "I

didn't disregard anything. And if you really wanted to keep him safe, maybe you shouldn't have hooked up with Dryden Kane's son in the first place."

He thought she brought this on herself? On Ethan? He thought they deserved this? Her legs shook. Her hands balled into fists.

She tried to breathe, tried to control herself. "I want those cameras out of here. I'm going to get Ethan." She'd call Detective McCaskey the moment she and Ethan got to their room.

She turned back to the pool, expecting to see Ethan at the bottom of the slide.

He wasn't there.

A jolt of panic raced along her nerves. Ridiculous. She'd seen him just a second ago. She'd only taken her eyes from him for a moment. He had to be here.

She scanned the wet heads and slick bodies of kids splashing, scampering and sliding.

No Ethan.

Her heartbeat grew faster, thumping in her ears. She ducked around concrete palm trees. She raced across the deck of the pool, dodging children, circling tables. She had to stay calm. Had to find her son.

A pair of black swim shorts with orange flames licking up the sides caught her attention.

Ethan. He stood on the other side of the pirate ship, just behind one of the smaller slides.

Her knees flagged with relief. Willing her trembling legs to carry her, she started across the pool area toward him. "Ethan?"

He was too far away and the pool area was too loud. He would never be able to hear her. He stepped away from the slide, toward a group of tables and chairs gathered around the entrance to the hotel lobby and atrium. Nodding his head, he seemed deep in conversation with a redheaded man.

A man who looked strangely familiar.

Panic rose in her throat like bile. She tried to control herself, tried to get a grip. The man talking to Ethan had red hair and a beard. There was no reason for her to be afraid. No reason for her to panic.

"Ethan!" Her shriek mixed in with the laughs and yells of children and disappeared in the constant roar of fountains. She started running, dodging scampering children, circling the first pool.

The man looked up, focusing on her with blue eyes. Eyes so much like Ethan's. Eyes so much like Cord's. Yet eyes that glinted cold and hard and emotionless.

Dryden Kane put his hand on Ethan's arm.

A scream rose in her throat. Surfaced to her lips. She had to reach Ethan. She had to save her son. Her baby.

The water park stretched forever, an obstacle course of pools and children and concrete jungle plants. She was so far away. Too far away.

"Kane!" A voice boomed through the room. Not hers. Not the cop's.

Cord's.

He burst into the water park through one of the lobby doors and stormed past Melanie. He raced for Ethan, raced for Kane. "Get away from him, you bastard!"

Chapter Five

Cord raced across the pool deck, circling tables and dodging children. He'd never seen Kane in person before, but he had no doubt the man with the cropped red hair and beard was him. Even from across the indoor water park, the bastard's eyes shone with an icy light. Inhuman.

Kane gripped Ethan's arm. Speaking in the boy's ear, he pulled him back from the kiddie pool, back toward the door to the hotel atrium.

Cord ran faster, skirting the center pool.

A little girl darted in front of him.

He slammed on the brakes and ducked to the side. Scrambling, he kept his feet under him and pushed on.

A scream rose from behind him over the din. Melanie. He couldn't make out what she was yelling, but he only hoped she was calling for a cop.

He kept running. He couldn't look back. If he

took his eyes from Ethan, he might not see which door Kane exited. He might lose his son.

Kane ducked behind a group of fake palms. Light reflected off glass. A door opening.

Cord dodged around the edge of the kiddie pool and made for the door Kane and Ethan had exited. He yanked it open and raced into the hotel.

The center atrium rose a dozen stories in the air. Each floor opened to a balcony rimming the circumference of the hotel. The center separated into restaurant, bar and seating areas. And in the far corner a waterfall cascaded down several yards and tumbled over a silver sculpture.

Cord spotted Kane.

The killer pulled Ethan across the center of the floor and ducked behind a half wall of potted ferns.

Cord went after him. When he reached the ferns, Kane and Ethan were halfway across the span of the atrium.

Closing in on the elevators.

"Stop that man!" His voice echoed through the gaping space.

Several people turned curious faces his way, but no one moved to help.

Not that he'd expected it. He could only hope Melanie could get the cop's attention. He could only pray he could stay on Kane's trail. If the monster slipped away, Ethan was gone.

The distance between them closed. Now that Cord had room to run, he was gaining. Dragging a struggling Ethan, Kane couldn't move as fast.

Kane threaded a gap between a seating area and fake palms and circled the two glass elevators.

Right behind them, Cord reached the elevator just as the doors closed. He jammed his fingers between the panels and pulled. Inch by inch they parted. The empty elevator shaft.

He'd lost them.

No. He couldn't lose them. He wouldn't let Kane take Ethan.

Cord let go of the doors. He raced around to the other side of the elevator bank. Through the column of glass, he could see the elevator car rising. He could take the other elevator, follow them, but first he had to see what floor they stopped on.

The back of Ethan's head pressed against the glass. Still clutching the boy's arm, Kane turned to look out the glass elevator and over the atrium. His eyes met Cord's. The bastard's lips thinned into a smile.

"Where is he?" Melanie raced toward him.

Cord didn't wait for her to reach him. He took off for the other elevator. He'd give Kane something to smile about. "In the elevator. Tell me which floor they get off on."

She looked up to the glass elevator and clasped her hand to her mouth. "Hurry."

Cord circled back to the elevator doors and jammed the button with a fist. The door of the other elevator slid open. Jumping on, he hit the button for the top floor. The elevator closed and started its climb. He looked out the glass, the lobby falling away beneath him. Focusing on Mel, he waited for her signal.

She met his eyes and held up nine fingers.

He hit the button for the ninth floor.

Each floor ticked by, one after another. Slowly. Too slowly. This damn elevator was taking too long. Kane could have taken Ethan anywhere by now.

Finally the elevator slowed to a stop. The floor number flashed on the digital screen, then held.

The eighth floor.

The door furled open. A smiling older couple stepped forward to board.

"You can't get on." Cord jammed the ninth-floor button. The last thing he needed were innocent bystanders in the way when he confronted Kane.

"I beg your pardon?"

Cord offered his best *Murder One* glare. If there was ever a time to look like a crazy and dangerous ex-con, this was it. "Get the hell back. This elevator is mine."

Identical expressions of horror streaked across their faces. They recoiled just as the door closed.

The elevator car resumed its climb. The door opened, this time on the ninth floor.

Cord lunged out of the elevator, fists up and ready.

The hall was empty in either direction. He circled the elevator bank and looked over the balcony.

Mel stood just where he'd left her. She pointed to the left.

Cord ran in the direction she'd indicated. His pulse throbbed in his ears. He reached the corner of the rectangular atrium.

"Cord!" Melanie's scream rose above the din below.

He located her racing across the lobby below, pointing back in the direction of the elevator.

Damn. Kane had taken the stairs to the floor above and doubled back.

Cord did a 180. If he could reach the elevator in time, he might be able to force the car to stop on his floor.

Lungs screaming for breath, he raced to the doors and hit the button. The light above the door lit. The bell dinged. The elevator slid open.

Cord met the eyes of Dryden Kane.

The monster stood behind Ethan. One hand gripped the boy's shoulder, the other held a knife to his throat. One sharp move and Ethan was dead. "Hello, son."

Cord looked at his own son. Ethan's eyes puddled with tears, but his cheeks were dry. Teeth clenched, he thrust his chin forward like a little soldier.

"Let him go," Cord said.

"I'm glad you could make it, Cordell." Low as a whisper, Kane's voice rang emotionless, flat. As if threatening to slit his grandson's throat was as significant to him as swatting a mosquito.

Cord jammed his foot in the corner of the elevator door track, preventing the door from closing. "The cops are here. The building is sealed off. There's no way out."

"Sealed off? By the time this place is sealed off, I'll be long gone." He tilted his head. "I just wanted to talk to the boy. I didn't count on you being here. But since you are, this gives us a nice opportunity to chat. An opportunity no father should pass up."

Cord studied the killer's face. The eyes so much like his. The slightly weaker jaw. The sharp cheekbones. He didn't want to chat with this man. He wanted to take that knife from his hand and jam it between his ribs. He wanted to remove him from the face of the earth and erase all evidence he ever existed. He wanted to forget this monster's blood flowed in his veins.

If only he could.

"The cops will be on this floor any second." At least he hoped they would be. He prayed.

"You're too smart for this, Cordell. Helping the cops?" Kane shook his head, as if sorely disappointed. "They sure as hell aren't going to help you. They'd just as soon see you back in the penitentiary."

Cord couldn't argue with that. He didn't even try. "There's no way out, Kane."

"There's always a way out."

"Not this time."

"Why do you listen to them, Cordell?"

Cord shook his head. He didn't listen to the cops. At least he didn't believe them. But he sure as hell wasn't going to believe anything Kane said, either.

"They tell you that you're scum. Dirt. They tell you that you're nothing. Why do you listen?"

"Let the boy go."

"I understand you, Cordell. Not the cops. Not Melanie Frist. *Me.* Do you know why?"

He didn't want to hear this. His hands ached to wrap around Kane's throat, to choke the life out of him. Whatever it took to shut him up.

The blade glistened hard and lethal against the tender skin of Ethan's throat.

"You're like me, Cordell. You share my blood." He looked down at Ethan and smiled. "Strong blood."

Cord ground his teeth together.

The smile widened. "But more than blood, you have tasted my power. The power over life and death."

Cord gritted his teeth until his jaw ached. As much as he didn't want to acknowledge he was anything like his father, Kane was right. They shared the same blood. And they were both killers.

"Why fight it? Others are weak. *They* are the ones who are nothing. Not us, Cordell. Not us."

Cord couldn't listen to this. "Let him go."

"No one understands that power until they've felt it. Until it burns inside. Until it consumes everything else. We know what it's like to hold life and death in our hands. We know what it's like to be God."

"Go to hell, Kane."

Shouts sounded from the first floor of the atrium.

The cops. It was about damn time.

Kane tilted his head, hearing the shouts, too. "I'll be in touch." He reached out with his knife hand to hit a button on the elevator panel.

Cord lunged forward. Grabbing Ethan's arm with one hand, he chopped down on Kane's with the other, breaking his grip. Cord enveloped the boy in his arms. He pulled Ethan away from Kane, out of the elevator.

To safety.

The elevator door slid shut.

SHOUTS AND FOOTFALLS echoed in the back of Melanie's mind like sounds from another world, another life. Her vision narrowed. All she could focus on was the glass elevator. All she could see was Kane's dyed hair. All she could think about was Ethan.

Her baby.

She didn't know what had happened to Cord. She hadn't seen him since she'd directed him back to the elevator. Now the elevator hung on the ninth floor.

"Ma'am? You have to leave this area. You have to come with me."

Her mind registered the officer's voice, the dark blue of his uniform. She shook her head. "My son is up there. You have to save my son."

"We will. But you have to clear out of here. It's for your own safety."

She glanced around the atrium. Officers scrambled into place. The SWAT team in their protective gear, snipers, all of them aiming to take Kane down. "You can't shoot him. My son is up there. You might hit my son." And Cord. What had happened to Cord?

He grasped her elbow in one hand and her fingers in the other. He started walking her away from the elevator.

She tried to pull back, to break away. She

couldn't. The more she fought, the greater pressure seized her arm.

"You have to move out of the way. You have to let us do our jobs. We won't hurt your son. Don't worry."

How could he tell her not to worry? How could he force her to leave when Ethan needed her?

Above their heads, the elevator car started descending. She could no longer see Kane inside. The car looked empty.

"He's not there! What happened?"

The officer increased his pace, forcing her to move with him, to walk farther and farther from her son. He half dragged her behind a planter on the edge of the atrium. SWAT officers moved into place, surrounding the doors.

The elevator passed the third floor. The second. It reached the lobby. Kane nowhere to be seen. It kept going, sinking to the lower level until nothing but its ornate copper roof showed above the lobby's tile.

Shouts rang out around her. "He went to the parking level! Are they set up yet?"

"No time!"

"How the hell did he bypass this floor?"

"Seal off the garage from the outside!"

The shouts and movement washed over her, blending with the thunder of her pulse in her ears, the fear buzzing in her blood. Above, the second car started its descent.

"The other one's coming down! Get into position!"

Blue uniforms surrounded the elevator doors.

The glass car lowered. Broad shoulders filled the clear upper half of the elevator. Sandy-brown hair. Tattooed arms.

Cord.

Melanie struggled to break free from the officer holding her arm. She had to reach Cord. She had to know what happened to Ethan.

The elevator came to a halt on the lobby level. The chime rang. Weapons leveled on the car. The doors slid open.

Melanie's breath seized in her throat.

Cord stepped out. And in front of him, shoulders braced by his father's hands, was Ethan.

Melanie broke free. Racing to the elevator, she fell to her knees and gathered her baby in her arms. He felt so solid, so warm, so alive. She scooped in breath after breath of his chlorine-scented hair. Her vision blurred, turning the world into a mosaic of watery color.

Through her tears, she looked up and into Cord's eyes—the eyes of the boy she'd once known. The boy she'd once loved. The man who'd saved her son. A cold shiver started in the pit of her stomach and spread over her.

"HE WAS IN THAT first elevator. So how in the hell did he get away?" Cord eyed Officer Herns, the cop assigned to protect Melanie and Ethan in the first place. The cop who was conveniently missing when Kane showed.

The cop avoided his gaze.

McCaskey cleared his throat, bringing Cord's attention to him. "SWAT didn't have time to set up. Probably the way Kane planned it."

"No 'probably' about it." He'd told Cord he'd be gone before the hotel was sealed. He hadn't been lying. "Why didn't the elevator stop at the lobby? Didn't anyone think to push the button?"

"He stole a key from an open maid closet. The key was still in the control panel."

Detective Valducci nodded like a bobble-head doll. "Kane is meticulous in his planning. He doesn't mess around."

"That's right." Detective Perreth lounged on the hotel room bed flipping an unlit cigarette in his fingers. "But the bottom line is that if you had held him up a little longer, we could have stopped him."

Cord couldn't believe what he was hearing. Even after the cops screwed up, the blame came down on *his* head, same as ever. At least for once he didn't deserve it.

He focused on McCaskey. "I have to talk to you."

McCaskey arched a dark brow. He gestured to the door with a nod.

"No, here." If the cop responsible for protecting Mel and Ethan was the one who'd leaked their location to the press, or worse to Kane, Cord wanted him to know he was on to him. He wanted to see the expression on the guy's face.

He could guess what Perreth's motive might be. The tension between him and McCaskey was palpable. Perreth would probably do a lot of things in order to undermine McCaskey. But Officer Herns wasn't so easy to read.

Perreth's grumble drifted from the bed, something about a punk-ass convict. The guy was a regular laugh a minute.

McCaskey focused on Cord. "Go on."

"Someone told the media that Ethan's my son. They also released his location. Someone in the police department."

Silence hung heavy in the room. Neither Officer Herns nor Detective Perreth made a move.

Unfortunately, neither looked overly guilt-ridden, either.

McCaskey nodded, as if this wasn't a surprise, as if he'd expected it. "Got a name?"

"No."

"You're sure it's a cop?" McCaskey asked.

"Sure enough to worry that this might not be a one-time thing. Melanie and Ethan aren't safe. And neither is Diana or her sister." Cord waited, sizing up McCaskey's reaction to the mention of his wife.

A muscle flexed along McCaskey's jaw. "Ideas?"

Nikki Valducci pushed her pretty face into the circle of men. "We use the leak to set a trap for Kane."

A bad feeling crept up Cord's spine and lodged like an ache in his shoulder muscles. "In order to set a trap, you need bait."

Nikki nodded. "But that doesn't mean anyone would be in danger. Not really. The key is to be pro-active instead of reactive. We plan as carefully as Kane. First we get everyone in place ahead of time."

"Nikki…" Reed's voice growled low in warning.

Valducci pushed on. "When their where-abouts leak and Kane shows up, this time we'll be ready for him."

"Forget it, Nikki," McCaskey said.

"It could work."

"It's too dangerous."

Cord had to agree with McCaskey there. After what had happened tonight, he wasn't going to let anyone put Mel and Ethan in danger again, no matter how brilliant the plan or well-meaning the planner.

"We could talk to Diana. She likes taking risks. And she just might like another visit with Daddy." Perreth gnawed on the filter end of his cig and shot McCaskey a challenging look that was clearly less about the plan to catch Kane and more about the sharp edge of tension stretching between the men.

McCaskey eyed Cord and nodded in the direction of the door that led into the adjoining room. "Come with me."

Cord hesitated. Something about his tone made Cord uneasy.

The detective's look grew impatient. "I have an idea. But I want to run it by you first."

Him? The bad feeling sunk its roots a little deeper, hitting bone. He forced himself to take a few steps in McCaskey's direction, winding around Perreth and past the suddenly quiet Officer Herns.

McCaskey rapped his knuckles on the door to the adjoining room, then glanced back at the cops in the room. "Nikki? You too."

A smile graced the cover-girl lips. McCaskey clearly didn't like her plan. But even Cord had to admit that among all the cops in the room, she appeared to have some smarts to go along with her eagerness. And with Mel and Ethan's safety on the line, he was starting to like the idea of an attack dog on the case.

As long as McCaskey was holding her leash.

The door to the other room opened. Melanie stared at them with bloodshot but relieved eyes, tracks of tears still visible on her cheeks.

Cord could still see her face when he'd delivered Ethan into her arms. He'd forgotten how powerful coming through for her had made him feel. How invincible. As if his entire life was justified in that split second. Standing at the elevator doors watching her hold Ethan tight against her heart had brought the feeling back. A feeling more addictive than any drug.

"We were just deciding what to do next," McCaskey said. "I thought you should be part of the discussion."

"I appreciate that." Leaving the door open, she retreated to a spot beside the bed and gathered Ethan into her arms.

Ethan's cheeks were as tear streaked as Mel's. But as the three of them filed into the room, he raised his chin, as if to show he was bowed but not broken. That he'd live to fight again.

Cord shifted his weight from foot to foot, trying to dislodge the feeling of pressure in his chest.

McCaskey focused on Mel. "We're going to need to talk about this alone. Do you mind if your son steps into the other room with Nikki?"

Nikki Valducci took a step backward. Judging

from the look on her face, she'd assumed Mc-
Caskey had called her into the room to hear more
about her proactive theories for catching Kane,
not because he needed a babysitter.

She let out a deep sigh. "You want to come with
me? You should see my new hand-held. I just
downloaded some awesome games for it. Ever
play Texas hold 'em?"

Ethan looked up at his mother.

Melanie gave him a hug and met his eyes. "If
you don't want to go right now, the police will
wait. They won't mind."

Judging from the muscle still working along
McCaskey's jaw, he did mind. But the fact that
Melanie didn't really care brought a smile to
Cord's lips.

Ethan stepped out of Melanie's embrace. "I'll go."

Mel glanced at McCaskey. "It won't be too
long, will it, Detective?"

"It won't be too long."

Nikki ushered Ethan into the adjoining room to
corrupt him with the ways of poker and shut the
door.

As soon as they were alone, McCaskey clasped
his hands behind his back like a military officer
at ease and studied Mel and then Cord. "I've taken
Diana and Sylvie out of police protection. Sylvie's

husband, Bryce Walker, will be taking them to a location only they and I know about. No one else."

Cord nodded. "So it's true. There *is* a leak in the police department."

Melanie's gaze flew to McCaskey. "A leak? Is that how Kane found us?"

"The leak was to the news media. Kane likely heard about it through them."

"How do you know?"

"We don't. We're still investigating. In the meantime, the important thing is to make sure it doesn't happen again. That's why I'm taking everyone in the police department out of the loop until we can get some answers. Everyone but me."

It sounded like a good idea. But there was one detail McCaskey hadn't covered. One detail that made Cord very nervous. "If Bryce Walker is watching Diana and Sylvie, who will be protecting Melanie and Ethan?"

McCaskey's dark eyes drilled into him. "You."

Chapter Six

"Me?" Cord waved his hands in front of him, trying to wipe McCaskey's suggestion from the air. It was impossible. Him? Protect Mel and Ethan? Stay with them day and night? "No. Not me."

Melanie stepped toward McCaskey. Eyes that looked relieved a moment ago flashed with fire. With worry. "He's right. It's not going to work."

McCaskey let out an impatient breath. "I know it's not ideal. And I have no idea what has happened between the two of you. But until we make sure that leak is not coming from the police department, until we can nail it down, we're going to have to improvise."

"How about you, Detective?" Melanie splayed her hands in front of her, palms up. "Why can't you protect us?"

"I'll be working on finding the leak. And finding Kane. I barely have time to eat these days.

I'm not going to be able to be with you 24/7. And that's what you need."

Cord gave a reluctant nod. McCaskey was right. Even with a cop protecting Mel and Ethan, Kane had found a way to get to them. But while McCaskey couldn't watch over them every moment, neither could Cord. "How about your partner?" He still hadn't forgiven the attack dog for her trap idea. But from what he'd seen, she might have just what it took to beat Kane.

"Nikki has her hands full. She has special training through the FBI that makes her very valuable in this case. We need her on the search for Kane."

Mel paced across the floor, her arms crossed over her chest. She looked as if she wanted to scream. As if she'd do just about anything before agreeing to rely on Cord. Or have her son near him.

Cord shook his head. "It's not going to work, McCaskey. Period. You'd better think of another way."

The detective arched a black brow. "You and I might have a lot of differences, but I thought I'd figured out at least a little bit about you after seeing you take on Kane. Apparently I was wrong. Ethan is your son, man. How can you just walk away when he needs you?"

"I'm not walking away."

"What do you call it then?"

Melanie halted in her tracks. "You don't understand, detective. It's not what Cord wants or doesn't want. This is far more complicated than that. It isn't going to work. Plain and simple."

"Even if it is the difference between keeping your son safe and losing him?"

Mel took a step back, as if McCaskey's harsh words were a physical blow.

Cord balled his hands into fists by his sides. "I'm no cop. I'm no bodyguard. I'm not qualified to do this."

"You're plenty qualified." McCaskey's dark gaze skimmed Cord's shoulders and moved over the prison tats. "Police officers go through regular training to overcome their natural hesitation to killing another human being. From what I know about you, you don't have that hesitation."

"You want me to kill Kane?"

"If you need to act, you'll act."

"And you know this how? Because I've killed before?"

"Among other things."

The acidic bite of bile tinged Cord's mouth. He was qualified because of who he was. What he was. McCaskey wanted him to protect Mel and Ethan for the exact reason he *couldn't* be around his son. The exact reason he needed to stay as far away as possible.

Numbness seeped into muscle, into bone.

McCaskey offered a slow nod, as if trying to reassure him. "You've lived in a world of predators most of your life. You understand the rule of kill or be killed. You understand it without thinking. Without hesitating. Without regulation and procedure getting in the way."

Melanie bristled. "What are you saying, Detective? That you want to throw the law away, and you're enlisting Cord to help you do it?"

"Where Dryden Kane is concerned, yes."

Her elegant brows dipped over narrowed eyes. "You can't mean that."

"Your son was very lucky today. Next time he might not be. Or you might not be. I don't want there to be a next time."

"Obviously neither do I."

"But you don't like the idea of killing Dryden Kane?"

"I'd kill him with my bare hands if he threatened Ethan. But that's not what you're suggesting. You might not be saying it out loud, but you're suggesting Cord disregard the law. You're suggesting he commit murder."

"No, I'm suggesting that if Kane shows up, Cord makes sure he takes the monster out."

She shook her head, her dark hair lashing her cheeks. "I don't have a problem with that idea. But what you said before about Cord not having to let regulation and procedure get in the way. What did you mean by that?"

Reed raked a hand through his hair and blew out a long breath. He suddenly looked tired. Or maybe it wasn't fatigue drawing his face down, maybe it was regret.

"What happened?" Cord asked.

"I had the chance to kill Kane. In the prison when he was holding Diana. I wanted to kill him. I didn't have my weapon, but that wasn't what stopped me. Once I was in control, I pulled back. I went for the arrest instead of the kill. I could have ended it right then, but I didn't."

"You did the right thing," Melanie said.

"Did I?"

"It would have been murder if you'd killed him when you didn't have to. Right?"

"It would have been worth it."

Mel shook her head.

Cord knew what she was thinking. Mel believed in the rules. She believed that when you did the right thing, you were rewarded. It had worked for her. By following the rules, she'd been able to lift herself out of the life she'd known as a kid. The life he'd known, too. But she didn't understand that things didn't always work out that way.

Cord did. He'd seen it over and over. He'd lived

through enough of it himself. Times when he'd tried to do the right thing. Times when he'd been kicked in the teeth all the same. He agreed with McCaskey. And if it came down to a choice between Ethan's life and Kane's, Mel would agree, too.

"Enforcing the law is my life," McCaskey continued. "But I have to tell you that for the last two months, I haven't been able to get my decision out of my mind. I thought about it when I heard about the corrections officers killed in Kane's escape. I thought about it when I moved my wife into protective custody. And I thought about it tonight when I heard Kane had abducted your son. Every time I wished I hadn't hesitated. Every one of those times my hesitation either cost lives or came damn close. And with Kane still out there…"

Cord dragged a breath into tight lungs. He wished McCaskey hadn't hesitated, either. He wished Kane was dead. But as much as any of them wished, it didn't change a thing. Kane was still out there. And although Cord was still what he was—an ex convict, a murderer, a man who should never be a role model for a boy—maybe he could still help. Maybe he could protect his son. "I won't hesitate."

McCaskey nodded. "Good."

Melanie's gaze bobbled, then dropped to the floor.

Cord focused on McCaskey. He had an idea, but

he needed the detective to make it happen. "I'll need a weapon, and I'll need it kept on the down low."

"I can get one for Melanie."

Cord nodded. As a felon on parole, he couldn't possess a gun. But Mel could. "Whatever works."

Melanie threw her hands in the air. "I don't want a gun. I don't want any part of this."

Cord kept his focus on McCaskey. Melanie might not want anything to do with him, but it couldn't be helped. "Also three cots, three sleeping bags, food and supplies."

"What do you have in mind? Camping?" Mel looked at him as if she thought he was crazy.

Maybe he was. But crazy or not, he wasn't going to let her down this time. He couldn't live with himself if he did. "Camping with a state-of-the-art security system."

MELANIE SHIFTED on the bench seat of Cord's small pickup, trying to negotiate around the stick shift without crowding Ethan's legs too much.

Or worse, brushing against Cord's.

Exhausted after all that had happened, Ethan leaned heavily against her. He lowered his head to her shoulder, then jerked awake, only to nod off again seconds later.

She couldn't believe this was happening. That

after cutting all ties with Cord ten years ago for Ethan's sake, he was now back in their lives. Full-time.

She trapped her hands between her knees, taking up as little room as possible in the cramped middle of the seat. Keeping still, she tried not to jostle Ethan out of his latest nod.

Whether she liked it or not, she had to admit McCaskey had a point. After watching the ferocity with which Cord went after Dryden Kane at the hotel, she knew he would do whatever needed to be done if Kane threatened them again. He'd protect them from any physical threat, that was certain. But it was the emotional threat he posed that worried her. The emotional threat to Ethan.

And to her.

She didn't think it possible after all that had happened between them, but when he'd emerged from that elevator with Ethan, she'd wanted to fling herself into his arms. She knew the feeling was caused by gratitude. How could it not be? He'd saved her baby, the most important part of her life. But there had been something more there, too. Old feelings. Feelings she'd tried so hard to kill. Feelings she thought she had.

Cord glanced at her as he shifted into third, blending with the speed of traffic. Shadow cupped his jaw, the dim green glow of dashboard gauges and the rhythmic pass of streetlights high-lighting sharp cheekbones and strong nose. "What are you thinking?"

The cold shiver that had started at the hotel rippled through her once again. "Nothing."

"This is going to be a long few days if that's all you're willing to say."

She didn't want to pour out her thoughts to him. She doubted he wanted it, either. Still she owed him something. He'd rescued Ethan, after all. "I don't know. I guess I was thinking about the hotel. About how you saved Ethan."

"I guess I was lucky they didn't mistake me for Kane in that elevator." His tone was light, but she could sense a touch of bitterness below the surface. Whether it was directed at Kane or the police, she couldn't tell.

She let her gaze move over his face. The resemblance was amazing. If she'd paid more attention to the news, she probably would have seen it before this. Or maybe not. Cord's features might be like Kane's, but the spark in his face, the warmth in his eyes made them come alive in a way Dryden Kane's never did. "How can you take that? Having someone mistake you for Kane?"

He lifted one shoulder in a shrug. "For the past two months, every morning when I shave, I look at

Dryden Kane in the mirror. It's either take it or quit shaving." He gave her a quick glance and a smile.

She didn't smile back. She couldn't manage to lift the corners of her lips if it meant her life. She focused out the window, on the street ahead. "I don't think you look anything like him. Not really."

Quiet hung heavy in the truck in the wake of her comment. No sound but the hum of tires on pavement broke the stillness. Cord stopped at a red light. She could feel him turn to her. "Are you sure you're comfortable? You look wedged in."

Comfortable? Not exactly. But her discomfort had little to do with the seating. "I'm fine."

"Maybe Ethan should sit in the middle."

"He's sleeping. Besides I told you, I'm fine." Even if he was awake, she didn't want Ethan to sit in the middle of the seat. The thought of him anywhere near Cord made her stomach seize.

It didn't make sense. She knew that. It wasn't that she thought Cord would hurt him. Far from it. He'd saved their son. But she just couldn't think of the two of them together, as if Cord's path in life would rub off on Ethan if they brushed each other in the truck seat. It was risky enough to sit next to him herself. "Where is this place we're going?"

"Along Lake Mendota."

"Where exactly?"

"We'll be there in just a minute, if that's what

you're asking." His gaze crowded her. His body heat filled the truck's cab.

She glanced through the back window at the pile of equipment and towels crowding the truck bed and piling up the sides of the topper. She'd probably be more comfortable in the midst of that pile of junk than sitting so close to Cord.

She shifted again on the bench seat. "Is there plenty of room at this place? I mean, Ethan and I are used to living alone. We like our privacy."

Cord's lips settled in a resigned line. Turning his attention back to the light as it turned green, he accelerated across the intersection. "You'll have plenty of privacy. Believe me, you'll hardly know I'm there."

She doubted that. Her body seemed to be in tune with his every glance, his every move. She'd felt that way since she'd first walked past him at the high school entrance, the quintessential bad boy leaning against a post with a cigarette dangling from his lips. Her obsession with him had only grown from there, until she was convinced she could change him, help him escape his desperate life. Until she really believed he wanted to get out of that neighborhood as much as she did.

Cord took the next left. The truck crested a hill and the lake opened before them, waves sparked by the moon and city lights. Against the dark gleam loomed the flat hulks of buildings.

Cord nodded to the shoreline. "Here's the place."

She scanned the structures ranging from three to six stories, jutting up from the shoreline. "It's a building?"

"I promised a security system, remember?" He drove down the dead-end street until he reached the parking lot at the very end. Solid brick reached six stories into the sky. Black windows stared down at them like dead eyes.

"It looks vacant."

"It is." He brushed past her legs and opened the glove compartment. Withdrawing a remote, he pressed the button and the door to the building's underground garage began to lift.

Her leg tingled where he'd touched. She gripped her thighs, digging her fingertips into her own flesh. She couldn't wait for that door to open. Couldn't wait to get into the building. Anything had to be better than sitting so close to him, the past teasing at the back of her mind. The worry of the present riding heavy on her shoulders.

As Cord drove into the partially underground garage, she twisted to Ethan and moved a hand to his thigh. It was time to wake him. She hated to do it, but he was too big for her to carry anymore, and she wasn't about to let Cord do it. "Ethan? We're here."

His body jerked. A whimper caught in his throat.

She circled his shoulders with an arm and held him close. "It's okay. You're here with me, honey. You're safe."

He blinked and focused on her.

"We just need to go inside. Then you can go back to sleep."

He nodded.

She hugged him close again. She could only hope and pray this would be over soon, before it took too much of a toll on Ethan. Or her.

The headlights illuminated dirt-tracked concrete and construction equipment. Cord pulled into a parking space next to an elevator door.

Melanie had the door open before he pulled his key from the switch. The garage smelled dank and cool, like new concrete. With three of them, it didn't take long to load the supplies into the elevator. Melanie positioned herself between Cord and Ethan while Cord hit the button to the penthouse floor.

"What is this place?"

"It's a contract of mine. High-end condos. They're scheduled to go on the market the end of next week."

"High-end? Why the camping equipment?"

"The units are sold as empty shells. The new owners choose how they'll be finished."

As an ex-convict, how would Cord have anything to do with high-end anything? "What is it you do?"

"I'm a window washer. Self-employed. That's what all that gear in the back of the truck is for. Squeegees, drop clothes, buckets and towels. Shop-Vac. I do all the builder's window cleaning and construction cleanup. I'm contracted to have this place clean before they start showing the units. And then again after the interior is finished. Construction dust can ruin a lake view, you know."

The elevator opened into a cavernous space that smelled of chalky white drywall. On the far side of the room, black windows stared out at the lake. "You weren't kidding when you said they were empty shells. What about that security system?"

He stepped to a keypad next to the elevator and punched in a series of numbers. "Now the elevator is locked. It won't open on this floor. And if we want to see what's going on in the lobby, we just hit this." He hit a button, and the monitor above the keypad came alive with images of the main entrance.

"Why would they have a system like this if the condos aren't even finished?"

"Vandalism. And there's still work going on in the lower units. Construction equipment is valuable." Cord glanced from her to Ethan and back.

"If you want that privacy, you can try the area to the right of the great room. Eventually it will be the master bedroom."

She nodded, but somehow her feet wouldn't move. As uncomfortable as she felt being near Cord again, the thought of being alone terrified her.

"I'll stay out here. No one will get near you."

Heat tinged her cheeks. Dryden Kane might still be loose in the city, but he wasn't here. He couldn't hurt her, couldn't hurt Ethan.

Thanks to Cord.

She handed Ethan two of the sleeping bags and picked up two cots. As her son started in the direction Cord had indicated, she met Cord's eyes. "Thank you."

His lips twitched into a frown. He waved off her gratitude.

"Really. Thank you for doing this. And for tonight. For saving Ethan."

"You don't have to thank me, Mel."

"Yes, I do." She couldn't even think about what would have happened had Cord not shown up. He might have devastated her in the past. He might have let her down, let himself down. She could never truly trust him again. But he'd come through for her tonight. He'd come through for Ethan. And that was worth all the thanks she could give. "I really appreciate it. More than you can know."

His lips twitched again. "It's the least I can do. Don't you think?"

"Mom?"

Shaken, she turned away from Cord, the possible meaning behind his words buzzing in her mind. "I'm coming, Ethan." She hurried to catch up to her son.

The bedroom area was an empty shell of bedroom and bath and closet space waiting to be allocated by walls. One end of the room opened into a solarium, the glass walls and ceiling filled with the swaying shapes of treetops rustling against a lighter sky.

She spread out the cots in the area farthest from the solarium's black glass and unrolled one of the sleeping bags for Ethan.

"Mom?" Ethan opened his mouth wide in a yawn.

"Yes, honey?"

"Is it okay if I just go to sleep? I don't have to brush my teeth or anything, do I?"

She was sure Ethan was tired. It had been a long day, and with all that had gone on, it was already past midnight. She also knew that he probably just needed to shut out the stress of the day. At least for a few hours. "I think you can get away with not brushing this once."

She unzipped the sleeping bag a few inches and turned it back, trying to keep her mind occupied with making Ethan's bed and not with Cord's comment. She pulled out one of the pillows from the bag of supplies and dropped it on the cot.

Ethan climbed in. Pulling the sleeping bag to his chin, he closed his eyes. "Will you stay with me? At least until I fall asleep?"

"Of course. I'll be here all night." She sank onto her cot. Ever since Ethan was born, she had loved watching him sleep. But tonight she needed it. "Do you want me to rub your back?"

"No, that's okay."

She wanted to touch him. To hold him close. To convince herself he would be all right. She folded her hands in her lap.

Tears surged at the backs of her eyes, tears she didn't know she still had in her. Swallowing hard, she forced them back.

"Mom?"

She hadn't known he was still awake. "Yes, Ethan?"

"You don't have to worry. Cord will keep us safe. I know he will."

She'd like to believe that. But after Cord's comment about this being the least he could do, she couldn't help but wonder if somewhere in his mind he had an idea of what the most might be. And the desire to fulfill it.

Chapter Seven

Cord looked up from the cot where he stretched out, his chest bare. Thick lines of tattoos etched the contours of muscle and marred smooth skin. "Can't sleep?"

Trepidation shot through Melanie. She'd spent the last hour listening to the gentle sound of Ethan's breathing, trying to push Cord's comment from her mind. But she'd had about as much luck as she was now having keeping her eyes off his bare chest. "What you said before was bothering me."

"And what was that?" He sat up and swung his legs over the side of the cot.

"I think it would be a good idea to set things straight." Crossing her arms over her breasts, she leaned back against the doorjamb. She needed the support. "You can't suddenly step into Ethan's life and be his father. He has a good life. He doesn't—"

"Need me?" Cord rose to his feet. He crossed

the room toward her. The shadows of individual windowpanes scrolled over his bare arms and chest as he walked, morphing and changing the tattoos. "I know. I don't belong near a kid. I don't need you to tell me that."

"Then what was your comment about? That this was the least you could do?"

"Just that." He stopped ten feet from her. "I'll never be much of a father, and I don't want him using me as some kind of role model any more than you do. But I can keep my son safe. I can kill Kane if he shows his face. You don't need to thank me for doing the one thing I can. It really is the least I can do. I wish I could do more."

She bit down on the inside of her lip. Maybe she shouldn't have thanked him for saving his own son. But since she'd first learned she was pregnant, Ethan had been hers and hers alone. Thinking of him as also being Cord's son would take getting used to.

She caught herself. She wasn't going to get used to it. Cord wasn't going to be in Ethan's life long enough. "I'm sorry. But I'm glad we had this talk. I'm glad we understand each other."

"We do."

She lowered her lids and rubbed her fingers over her forehead, suddenly so tired she could hardly stay upright. It would be hard to get through these next days holed up in this shell of a condo with Cord, but she could do it as long as she knew that Cord would walk away when it was over. That Ethan would be okay in the long run.

And that she'd be okay, too.

When she opened her eyes, Cord was staring at her. The intensity of his blue eyes sparked a tremble high in her stomach. "What?"

He blew a derisive laugh through his nose and shook his head. "I've thought about what I'd say to you for the past ten years."

She didn't want to hear what he had to say. "Cord…"

"I rehearsed it. Honed it. Even though I never planned to actually say any of it."

"I don't think we should talk about this."

"Why not? If Kane hadn't included your name in his invitation, you never would have seen or heard from me. But he did. And I can't pretend you're not standing here in front of me now."

"I don't want to hear it. I can't." She turned, the need to get back into the room with Ethan almost overwhelming.

"Wait, Mel. Please. I need to explain."

She held up a hand. "No, you don't."

"I want you to understand why I had to break my promise. Why I went to head off Snake that night."

She shook her head. She'd avoided visiting him in jail for a reason. She hadn't wanted to hear the explanations. She hadn't wanted to hear the excuses. Once he started talking, she hadn't been sure she could have walked away. And she'd had to walk away. She'd had to escape from that life. She couldn't let her feelings for Cord trap her in a lifetime of violence and desperation.

The life her mother had lived.

She turned back to face him. "I'm sure you had your reasons. But that doesn't mean I have to stand here and listen to them. All the reasons in the world don't change a damn thing."

"I know it doesn't change anything. Believe me. I just—"

"You just what? Want to tell me what a good reason you had for killing Snake? I grew up in the same neighborhood, remember? I know what a scumbag Snake was. I know what he was capable of. I'm sure Detective McCaskey would have applauded you for what you did. Of course, he still would have thrown you in jail."

"Snake was making noises about Leon. He went at Leon with a knife. I had to stop him."

Of course he did. Cord had always been the leader of that rag-tag gang. They weren't the Crips or the Bloods. They hadn't killed people for points or run drugs. They'd been a mixed-race group of misfits that didn't belong anywhere else. And Cord had taken care of them, protected them, bailed them out. "You should have let Leon take care of himself."

"Leon? You must be joking. He wouldn't have lasted ten minutes, and you know it."

She held up her hands, as if she could block all of it with her palms and push it away. "Then Leon should have called the police."

"You know that wasn't an option. Not for Leon."

"Or for you." She blew out a strong breath and shook her head. Suddenly her anger and frustration seemed to burn out, leaving nothing but drab gray ash. Cord still didn't get it. Not after all the years in prison. "I don't think you did what you did for Leon at all."

"What are you saying?"

"I think you rushed in to save Leon for your own sake. Just the way you stood up for the rest of the gang. Because protecting them, leading them and being worshiped by them made you feel powerful."

Cord let out a bitter laugh.

"What's funny?"

"Nothing. I was thinking about Kane."

She wasn't following. "Kane?"

"He told me almost the same thing."

"When?"

"Tonight. In the elevator before I got Ethan away from him."

She leaned toward him. "What did he say?"

"That I was like him. That killing made me feel powerful. Like a god."

A bitter taste filled her mouth. "Did it?"

He shook his head. "Killing Snake felt like I was killing myself."

She let his words hang in the air, unsure what to say. His actions had killed her, shattered her heart, destroyed her dreams. Left her all alone to raise their son. But she'd survived. She'd risen from the ashes and brought Ethan with her. And she wasn't going back to that place.

Never again.

"The gang didn't make me feel powerful, Mel. You did. The way you used to look at me. The way you believed in me."

Chills peppered her skin. She should probably feel more, but she didn't know what. Not devotion. Not love, after all that had happened. Certainly not trust. She had gone through so much ten years ago. She'd loved Cord more than she'd thought it was possible to love anyone. She'd believed in him utterly. And he'd thrown it all away. "Then why, Cord? If my belief in you was so significant, why did you destroy it?"

He pawed a hand over his face and let it fall limp to his side. "I don't know. I guess I just couldn't believe back."

She closed her eyes. She'd spent ten long years

wishing things hadn't happened the way they had. But wishing never changed anything. It was time she accept it and let go.

She opened her eyes and met his gaze. "That's exactly why you can't be around Ethan. I've brought him up to believe. And I want him to stay that way."

SUZANNE BELLE PULLED off her boring old suit and blouse and tried to think of what the hell to wear. Friday night out with the girls always gave her wardrobe envy, a condition that her addiction to shopping never seemed to cure. Whatever she chose to put on, another one of the gang was wearing something shorter or sexier or just plain better looking—in short, something that garnered more attention.

Slipping off her utilitarian bra and white cotton panties, she opened her lingerie drawer and plucked out her favorite, the red lace bra that made her breasts look at least one cup size bigger than they really were. At least she had good lingerie. That was a start.

Maybe she should build on that. Maybe her white see-through blouse would capture a little attention. Show off the red lace. It was worth a shot. God knew she didn't want to spend another night out drinking alone while her friends were on the dance floor.

She was about to slip it on when movement outside her window caught her eye.

She grabbed her suit jacket. Holding it in front of her to cover her nakedness, she peered into the darkness.

Sure enough, there was a peeping Tom standing on the rooftop deck of the new brick condos next door. She stepped to the window to get a better look.

She didn't usually go for guys with red hair and beards, but this one was pretty hot. Respectable looking, even, and respectable usually meant money. Maybe he wasn't a peeping Tom at all, but just a nice guy who couldn't keep from looking when the opportunity presented itself. The only problem was, he wasn't looking at her.

But he would be.

She let the jacket fall to the floor and stepped back from the window to give him a full-length view.

The bastard didn't even have the decency to notice. His attention was focused down at the building beneath him. Through the solarium window of the penthouse he watched as the shadow of a fully clothed woman paced inside.

Chapter Eight

Cord pulled the strip washer from his bucket and tilted it to the side, letting the excess window-cleaning solution run off into the bucket. When it faded to a trickle, he tilted the washer the opposite way and brought it to the glass.

He figured that while he was here, he might as well work. The prospect of just sitting around listening to every word or movement or breath from Melanie and Ethan was agony. Running over his discussion with Mel last night was torture.

After wetting the pane, he set the strip washer back in the bucket and pulled out his razor scraper. Flipping down the blade guard, he started scraping the manufacturer's sticker and other debris from the glass.

"Can I help?"

The voice was so quiet, at first he thought it

was his mind playing tricks. He spun around to face his son.

His son.

He'd turned the idea over in his mind all night, and still the fact he was a father stunned him. "Not a great idea."

"Why not?"

Because Cord had nothing to offer? Because kids shouldn't be hanging around ex-cons? Murderers? "Um, I don't think your mom would like it."

"She doesn't care."

Right. "Where is she?"

"Sleeping."

Cord had listened to the steady beat of her pacing all night. It was about time she got some sleep. And when she woke up, Cord could just imagine how happy she'd be to see Ethan kicking it with him. "You don't want to be hanging around me. I'm not much of a kid person."

"Do you have kids?"

Just a day ago, he could have said no. He wouldn't have known it was a lie. Things were different now. And the irony of his own son asking that question, and him having to lie to the boy to answer it, tasted bitter on his tongue. "No. I don't have kids."

"Then how do you know?"

"What?"

"How do you know you aren't a kid person?"

He almost had to laugh. It seemed Ethan inherited his mother's ability to back him into a corner with his own words. "I just do. Trust me."

Ethan leaned against the corner of the bay window. Balancing on one foot, he scratched his shin with an athletic shoe.

Cord tried to go back to scraping the window, but it was no use. All he could focus on was Ethan watching him. What did he see? What was he thinking? This wasn't going to work. "Go on, kid. Go back in the other room."

"Is it true? What Dryden Kane said?"

This conversation was going from bad to worse. Cord flicked the guard back on the blade and shoved the razor scraper in his tool belt. He turned and eyed the kid. "Dryden Kane is a bad man. You can't believe anything he says."

"I know who he is. I know he killed lots of people."

"Then why would you listen to anything he said?"

"He said you killed someone, too. Did you?"

The question hit like a kick to the head. Cord had lied a lot of times in his life. To his mother. To the cops. To the corrections officers and fellow inmates. Lying had never bothered him.

It did now. "I made a lot of mistakes. Mistakes you have no idea how much I regret making."

"Did you kill someone?"

"I don't want to talk about this, Ethan."

His eyes widened. "So you did?"

So much for ducking the question. "Your mom is going to wonder where you are."

"What was it like? Did you go to jail?"

"Listen, I'm not answering your questions. Got it? So back off."

The kid's face flushed pink. He looked down at the floor.

Damn. Cord ran a hand over his cropped hair. Now he'd crushed the boy's feelings. He'd just been asking innocent questions—questions he couldn't help wondering about after witnessing Cord's little conversation with Kane in the elevator. And here Cord had jumped down his throat.

Exactly why he shouldn't have anything to do with the kid. "I'm sorry, kid."

Ethan nodded but didn't look up. He made a line in the dust with his shoe.

"It was a bad time in my life. I have a hard time talking about it."

Another nod.

He was getting nowhere. Ethan would never understand what Cord had gone through. At least, Cord hoped he never would. He should leave it alone. Quit talking. Let the kid slink away, hurt feelings and all. Let him hate Cord. Maybe then he'd steer clear the rest of their time in the condo. Maybe hurting the kid's feelings was the only way. The price Ethan needed to pay.

Cord rubbed a hand over his face. "If you want to help, you can pick up that strip washer and soak down this window."

The kid looked up. Hope beamed from his face like a new damn dawn. He reached down to the bucket and grabbed the handle. "I just rub this across the glass?"

"Yeah." He shouldn't be encouraging the boy. He shouldn't even be in the same room with him. But what was the alternative?

Ethan didn't deserve to have his feelings crushed for asking a simple question. No, Cord would let him wash a window then tell him to go back to his mother. Washing one damn window wasn't going to change anything.

Ethan carried the strip washer to the window Cord had just scraped and rubbed it over the glass until every inch was wet with solution. He looked up at Cord, his eyes as bright as if the chance to help was the most exciting gift he'd ever received. "Now what?"

Good question.

Cord tore his gaze from those blue eyes, so eager and fresh and so like his own. One window. That was it. "You wipe the top of the glass to make sure bits of sawdust don't get under the squeegee blade. Like this." Pulling out a cotton towel, he swiped the top of the pane.

"And then you squeegee?" Ethan pointed to the tool hanging from Cord's belt. "With this, right?"

Cord pulled the squeegee from his belt and handed it to Ethan. He guided the kid's hand to the window and fitted the rubber blade against the top of the glass. "Put it as close to the top as you can. Then pull straight down."

Ethan did as he said. The blade wove for the first few inches, then he managed to steady it and do a respectable job.

"You're a natural."

Ethan's lips stretched into a smile that beamed from his whole face. "Can you show me how to swoop the squeegee around?"

Cord knew he shouldn't be enjoying the look on Ethan's face. He shouldn't be hanging on the excitement in his voice. But even knowing his mistake, he couldn't turn away. All he wanted to do was stand here and soak in the kid's enthusiasm like drunks soak in booze. "Swoop it around, huh?"

"Yeah, like the window washers do at mom's lab." He held the tool up in the air and swooped the blade around as if squeegeeing an invisible window.

Cord couldn't help but grin. All his memories

from his own childhood centered around his mother's indifference and the struggle for survival. He didn't have the chance to notice things like the techniques window washers used.

He liked that his son could. He liked it a lot. "We'd better pack this up. Your mom is going to wonder where you are."

"Can't you show me how they do that?"

He wanted to, more than he wanted to admit. But he couldn't. Cord shook his head. "We can't swoop it around on these windows. Not without getting streaks."

"Why not?"

"It's best to keep it simple with construction cleanup jobs. Otherwise you get paint specks or bits of sticker under the blade. That's where the streaks come from."

"Oh." Ethan was still smiling, but Cord could see the slight flicker of disappointment.

Oh, hell. "I'll show you on another job, another day."

"Cool."

Cord had no right to make such a promise. A promise that implied he and Ethan would have a future together, a future that could never happen.

He shook his head, disgusted with himself. He needed to get rid of his kid before he promised to coach his Little League game or some damn thing. "You'd better get out of here. Your mother will be worried."

Ethan narrowed his eyes, watching Cord through light blue slits. "Why don't you like me?"

"Like you? I like you."

"Then why do you want to get rid of me?"

Blowing the breath through tight lips, Cord shook his head. "I don't want to get rid of you, Ethan."

"Then why are you always telling me to go back in the room with Mom?"

"Because spending a lot of time together isn't a good idea."

"'Cause you think I'll get attached or something?"

"Something like that." And that Cord would get attached right back. "Sometimes things can't be the way you want them, kid. Sometimes you just got to accept the way things are."

Ethan nodded, as if he understood.

At least one of them did.

MELANIE GRIPPED the edge of the doorway. The tremble in her knees spread into her chest and hands. She should have stepped into the room as soon as she'd discovered Ethan talking to Cord. She should have put a stop to it. But somehow her feet wouldn't move. Somehow her voice wouldn't function.

It was the expression on Ethan's face that had stopped her.

Wielding that squeegee like a sword, he looked like the Ethan she knew. Carefree. Adventurous. As if he'd forgotten all about Dryden Kane and the scare they'd had the night before. As if he was back to being a normal kid. A kid enjoying time with his dad.

She only wished it was that simple.

She forced herself to release the wall and step into the room. She'd spent her life protecting Ethan. She couldn't let dreams that had died ten years ago stop her now. "Ethan?"

He jerked his head around, as if he'd been caught doing something he shouldn't. "I was just washing windows."

"That's fine. But now it's time to go back into the other room." She shot Cord the hardest look she could muster.

"But, Mom…"

"Come on." She forced shaking legs to carry her across the great room to the master bedroom area. She hated being the heavy. But Cord had been right to tell Ethan there were things in life he just had to accept.

A shuffle of rubber soles on plywood followed.

Safe inside the master bedroom, she sank onto her cot before her knees decayed into a quivering mass. If only the condo was finished off enough to have doors. She'd like to lock Ethan inside. "Sit."

"I have to go check the lake."

"The lake?"

"Yeah. There were some dark clouds. They might even turn into a thunderstorm. I want to see it come across the water."

Melanie frowned. She wished she could believe his interest in a storm was that strong. But she had the feeling that Cord held more appeal than any storm. "I know it's kind of boring holed up in this room. But you need to stay here with me."

"Why? It's just a storm. It's awesome."

If it was just a storm he wanted to see, she'd agree with the awesome factor. "You need to stop bothering Cord."

His shoulders straightened, as if he was squaring for a fight. "He doesn't think I was bothering him."

No. Though Cord had tried to talk Ethan into going back to the bedroom, the expression on his face was anything but annoyed. More like awed. And that's what worried Melanie most. "Whatever Cord thinks doesn't really matter. You need to stay with me."

"Why can't I talk to him?"

A muscle pinched at the back of her neck. "Because." She knew that would never satisfy him. Ethan had always needed an explanation ever since he could understand language. As long as he understood the why behind a rule, he would follow it without fail. And if he didn't understand, he would ask and argue until he did.

She braced herself.

"Cord is nice. He doesn't mind it when I talk to him."

"I mind."

"Why?"

What could she say? Because he's your father? Because he's been in prison? Because I don't want you following in his footsteps?

She latched on to what Cord had started to tell Ethan. "Because I don't want you to get too attached to Cord. He's not going to be around long."

Ethan plopped down on his cot. He glanced out the door, then picked up his Game Boy with a sigh.

Poor kid. He didn't understand what was going on, what was at stake. How could he? "You okay?" she asked.

"I guess." He switched on the game. A high electronic beeping filled the room. "It just makes me…"

Sad. Upset. She knew it without having to ask. But she voiced the question anyway. "Makes you what?"

His shoulders slumped. He started pushing the buttons with this thumbs, moving them so fast they looked like they were twitching. "You don't want to hear."

She stepped across the distance and lowered

herself to the cot beside him. She hated being the ogre. She'd never been good at it. And the thought of Ethan withdrawing again after seeing him come alive with Cord hurt like an open wound. "If it's something you think or feel, I want to hear it. Always."

He glanced up from the game. "It just makes me wish he was going to be around all the time. You know, like he was my dad or something."

She caught the gasp before it could escape her throat. Gripping her knees, she braced herself as the tremble worked through every muscle in her body. Since Ethan had stepped off the bus yesterday afternoon, she'd been so concerned with keeping him away from Cord, she hadn't even considered she might be too late.

MEREDITH UNGER LIKED her life. She should. She'd worked damn hard to transform herself from the mousy daughter of an assembly line worker into one of the most glamorous and sought-after attorneys in southern Wisconsin. And next year with the release of her first book, she'd take the leap onto the national stage. Life was good. Or so she thought until she stepped from the shower after a long day at work and looked into the ice-blue eyes of Dryden Kane.

"I need some legal advice."

Her pulse beat in her ears, drowning out the low tones of his voice. She'd known she was taking a risk when she agreed to represent him, but she'd thought that risk was political. A tradeoff between becoming a household name and some people despising her for her belief that even monsters should have basic human rights.

Never in her worst nightmares did she imagine her client would one day be standing in her bathroom.

His lips pulled back in a smile, revealing straight, white teeth. "I never thought you'd be tongue-tied, Meredith. You don't seem the type."

He was right. She wasn't the type. She was cool under pressure and always in control. She sucked in a breath of steam and tried to remember that. "I was just surprised. Why don't you make yourself comfortable? I'll get dressed, then we can talk."

He leaned back against the doorjamb and crossed his arms over his chest. "I'm comfortable."

Panic lapped at the edges of her mind. She had to concentrate. She had to stay calm.

She hadn't taken Kane's case lightly. She knew what he'd done. What he liked to do. She also knew it was the fear that turned him on. The screams. The utter dominance and control.

No one controlled Meredith Unger.

She swallowed into a tight throat. "Are you here to kill me, Dryden?"

"Kill you?" He ran his gaze over her bare skin. She clutched the towel tighter to her body.

"It's a nice idea, but I have a job for you."

"A job?"

"You still represent me, don't you?"

"Yes. Of course I do." She scooped in another breath. The air flowed easier this time. "And as your attorney, I have to advise you to turn yourself in."

"So I can go back to prison?"

"So you don't get killed. Police from all over the state are looking for you."

"You think too much of the police. A bunch of idiots."

"Idiots with guns."

He waved away the warning with the back of his hand. "I have more important things to worry about."

More important? "Like what?"

"Family. I'll go back to my cell if I must. But I want to see my family first. They're what really matters."

His family? He had to be joking. Or more likely, trying to twist her sympathy around his little finger until it was transformed into something unrecogniz-able. "What does your family have to do with me?"

"You represent me."

"As far as the law goes."

"You can represent me in this, too. I need to talk to my son."

"Cord Turner?"

He nodded. "I need him to convince my daughters to see me again. To smooth things over."

"Smooth things over?" The words were out of her mouth before she could stop them.

"You're surprised? Things get lonely in prison, Meredith." He stepped closer. Reaching out, he brushed a strand of wet hair from her cheek. "So lonely."

The cold of his fingers trickled into her blood. Stifling the shudder, she forced herself to stand very still, to not let him see the fear building in her like a tsunami heading for shore.

"Your visits always helped, of course, but in the end there's nothing like family. Nothing like a father's relationship with his little girls. Nothing like his camaraderie with his son. And his grandson." His lips thinned in a smile. "I want them back, Meredith. And I want you to help me."

"You tried to kill one of your daughters."

"I didn't say it would be easy."

She didn't even bother to point out last night's attempt to kidnap his grandson. He obviously wasn't in touch with reality.

Or maybe he was.

She'd learned that with Kane. That even when he seemed out of touch, he wasn't. When he seemed lost in some fantasy, it was only a calculated way to get what he wanted. Manipulation. Domination. Control.

Wanting his family back probably had nothing to do with his feelings for them. She doubted he even had feelings. More likely it was just Kane's way to win her cooperation so he could get his hands on his daughters, kill them, gut them, like he'd done to all those other women.

Like he probably wanted to do to her.

One thing was for sure. She'd feel better if she had more than a towel between her and this monster. Like maybe the police. "Why don't you let me get dressed, then we'll see what we can do."

His gaze scraped over her. "Go ahead."

"Could I have some privacy?"

"I'm disappointed in you, Meredith."

"Disappointed?" The look in his eyes crawled over her skin. "Why?"

"Asking for privacy when you really just want me to leave the room so you can call the police. If you want to get dressed, do it right now. Here in front of me. I promise I'll enjoy the show."

She let out a defeated breath. So much for that idea. She sure as hell wasn't going to dress in front of him. She'd do whatever it was he wanted in a towel. And then pray for him to leave her alive. "What do you want me to do?"

"Call my son."

"I don't know how to get ahold of him."

"He's your client, isn't he?"

"Ten years ago." A bit of trivia she'd never shared with Kane. "How did you know about that?"

"You think I chose you solely based on your qualifications?" He focused on the swell of her breasts at the top of her towel. Reaching to his belt, he slipped a knife from its sheath. The light over the vanity flashed on the blade. "Of course, if you won't call Cordell for me, I guess those qualifications are all you can offer."

She gripped the towel, hands shaking.

Kane leaned toward her. Starting at her shoulder, he moved his face along her collarbone and up her neck, taking in a long slow breath through his nostrils. "Mmm. Just the scent I like. Fear."

"Please."

"Call my son." He brought his eyes level with hers. His face was so close, she could smell the mint on his breath. He rested the knife blade flat against the top edge of her towel and pushed the terry cloth down.

She forced herself to think, to hang on to some shred of composure before panic swept her away. The news coverage had mentioned Cord owned a cleaning company of some kind. A cleaning company would advertise for clients. Perhaps in the yellow pages.

She gripped the towel firmly in her fists, stopping its descent at her waist. "Okay. I'll find a way to reach him. What do you want me to say?"

Chapter Nine

Cord punched the off button on his cell phone. He hadn't heard his former attorney's voice in ten years, but he couldn't shake the feeling that there was something strange about the way she sounded that went along with the strangeness of her request.

"Was that Reed?"

He looked up to see Mel standing in the doorway. How long she'd been listening, he didn't know. "No."

"Who was it?"

He didn't know how to explain the call to her. He wasn't sure what to think of it himself. "Meredith Unger. My former attorney."

"Your attorney?"

"And Kane's."

She frowned, a little crease digging between her eyebrows. "That can't be a coincidence."

"No."

"What did she want?"

"She was calling about Kane's little wedding reception. She had a few requests to pass along to me."

"Requests from Kane?"

"He wants me to pick up a few things."

"Like what?" She arched her brows. Her eyes flinched as if she was preparing for the answer. An answer she knew she wouldn't like.

"Flowers, a cake and, oh yeah, Diana and Sylvie."

"He wants you to bring your sisters to him? He'll kill them."

"I think that's the idea, yes."

"Why does he think you would carry out his orders?"

"Besides the fact that I'm a killer just like him?"

"Don't even joke about that."

"Who's joking? I told you what he said in the elevator."

"Yeah, that's what Kane said. But why does he think you'll do it?"

He didn't want to tell her that part. Melanie had enough to worry about, especially where Ethan was concerned. She didn't need more.

"You never answered my question. Why does he think you'll cooperate? Did he threaten you?"

"Not in so many words. But I'm sure whatever he has planned, it's nothing nice." Of course with Kane, that was a given.

The feeling he'd gotten when listening to Meredith Unger's voice washed over him again. He remembered her being such a forceful personality. Maybe it was because he was only eighteen at the time he'd met her, but she'd seemed so confident, flamboyant even. A woman who was larger than life. "She sounded scared."

Melanie pressed her lips into a line at the veer of topic. "Meredith Unger?"

"Yeah. Her voice sounded thin. Almost trembling."

"Having a client like Kane would be pretty scary."

"Not just that. I mean she sounded really scared. And maybe a little out of breath."

She scanned his face, as if trying to read what he wasn't telling her. A look of horror rounded her eyes. "You think Kane's giving her those instructions in person, don't you?"

Was that it? Was Kane with Meredith Unger right now? Was that what he'd heard in her voice? Panic? Desperation? "Yeah. Maybe."

He rested his free hand on the grip of the Glock McCaskey had given him.

Melanie looked down at the gun. "You're not thinking *you're* going to rush over and kill him?"

"No." It had been just a reflex, reaching for the gun. As much as he burned to take Kane out, he wouldn't leave Mel and Ethan. Releasing the gun, he pulled his cell phone from his belt and flicked it open.

"Who are you calling? McCaskey?"

Cord nodded. "I think he needs to check on my former attorney." He punched in McCaskey's cell number.

The detective answered on the second ring. "Yeah."

"Meredith Unger just called me."

"What about?"

"She sounded scared." He needed to tell Mc-Caskey the rest. The request for favors Meredith had made on Kane's behalf. The threat she'd dangled over his head to insure his compliance.

He eyed Mel. He couldn't tell McCaskey. Not over the phone. Not until he'd told Mel exactly what Meredith Unger had implied. Not until he'd leveled with her.

His first reaction had been to protect Mel, but he could see now that wouldn't work. She had to know what she faced. She had to be as prepared as Cord. It was the only way they could be sure to keep Ethan safe.

"Turner?"

He brought his attention back to McCaskey. "You might want to send someone over to her place. Like maybe a SWAT team."

"Right."

"And stop by here afterward. I'll fill you in on the rest." Cord cut off the call. He'd explain Kane's instructions to McCaskey then. Somehow he doubted the detective would like them any more than he did.

He clipped the phone back on his belt and focused on Mel.

"What?"

"Maybe you should sit down."

"There's more? More you haven't told me?" She whipped her head around, glancing toward the bedroom. Toward their son. "It's about Ethan."

"Yes."

"Kane threatened him."

"Yes." He swallowed, his throat so dry it burned. "Meredith asked if Ethan was coming to the reception. She wanted to know if he would serve cake."

Her cheeks paled, chalk white against her dark hair. She scooped in a deep breath as if sucking in courage. "What does that mean, serve cake?"

"He isn't going to touch Ethan, Melanie. I'm not going to let him."

"I know. I know you won't."

For a second Cord's chest seemed to swell. It felt so good to hear she believed in him. That she trusted him to protect their son. But he couldn't soak in the feeling. He couldn't let himself enjoy it. He had to focus. He had to come through.

And if he failed, he had to make sure Melanie could take up the slack.

Cord pulled out the pistol again and turned it over in his hands. "Have you ever fired a gun?"

She looked at him as if he wasn't making any sense. "No, of course not."

"You have to learn."

She held her hands up in front of her, as if shielding herself from the weapon. "No, thanks."

"If something happens to me, you need to be able to protect yourself. You need to be able to protect Ethan."

She closed her eyes. Her body swayed.

He couldn't let her shut him out. This was important. Surely Melanie could understand that. "We can't be unprepared. No matter what happens, we have to be ready. Do you understand what I'm saying?"

She opened her eyes and stared past him. Finally she nodded. "If you think it's necessary, I'll do it. I'll do whatever I have to."

MELANIE WAITED more than an hour until Ethan was settled in with his Game Boy, his earphones blocking all sound except the beeps and explosions and inane electronic tunes, before she made her way back to the entryway where Cord leaned against the wall.

"That took you long enough."

"I couldn't just leave. I don't want Ethan to know." Or be anywhere near the gun. If only she could stay far away from the thing, as well. "Let's get this over with."

He handed the pistol to her, grip first. "I unloaded it." He held up a cartridge and pulled back the slide to show her.

She didn't see any bullets inside, but then she probably wouldn't recognize one if her life depended on it. At least it wouldn't accidentally go off in her hands. But the thing still looked so cold and hard and downright evil, she had to swallow a surge of revulsion when her fingers closed around the handle.

The thing was cold but not as heavy as she'd guessed. She expected it to smell like the gunpowder in firecrackers, but it gave off a faint, oily turpentine smell instead. But as light as the smell was, it did nothing to calm her nausea.

"It's not alive. It can't bite you."

"Are you sure?"

"Here." Cord fitted it snugly into the web between her thumb and forefinger. The warm roughness of his touch spread heat up her arms.

She focused on the gun. As dangerous as the weapon was, it was safe compared to her reaction to Cord's touch and the memories it evoked.

Anything seemed safe compared to that. "Okay. What do I do with it?"

"Stand with your feet apart and one foot slightly back, so you're balanced." He brushed her thigh with one hand.

She shifted her feet to the position he indicated. "Okay. I put my finger here, right?" She touched the trigger with her index finger and flinched despite herself.

"Slow down. You're getting ahead of yourself. Never put your finger on the trigger until you're ready to shoot."

She jerked her finger off.

"Just put it alongside, like this." He guided her finger into place, stretching it out along the gun's barrel above the trigger. "Then when you're ready to shoot, you move it to the trigger."

"Okay." She looked down at her finger, studying the way it felt against the gun so she could remember.

He moved his hand to her right arm, pushing up on her elbow. "Hold this arm straight."

She straightened her arm.

"Then brace with your other hand, arm slightly bent. Put your left thumb over your right." He pretended to hold a gun out in front of him, modeling the posture instead of touching her this time.

Thank God. She mimicked the way he held his hands, folding her left thumb neatly over her right.

"Now lean forward, relax your shoulders, point at his upper chest and shoot."

Lifting the pistol high in front of her, she tilted her head to the side and closed one eye.

"Don't aim."

She lowered the gun. "How am I supposed to hit him if I don't aim?"

"Aiming is great if you had time to practice. You don't. If he's coming at you, he'll be on top of you before you line him up. Just point at his chest and shoot."

She raised the gun again, pointing through the long entry area, through the great room and out the long bank of windows, now dark.

"Too high. Here." He stepped up closer behind her. Circling an arm around either side of her, he guided her arms down. His chest pressed against her, pushing her upper body forward and her weight to the balls of her feet. "Now squeeze the trigger."

Her body tensed. She tried to focus on the gun, the windows on anything but the feel of his body against hers. The heat. The familiar scent. She jerked back the trigger with her finger. The gun wavered to the right. Her whole body flinched and shuddered.

Disaster.

"It's okay. Let's try it again."

It wasn't okay. Not the feel of the gun in her hand, not the invigorating sense of his body surrounding hers, not the tinny taste in her mouth. None of it was okay. "I don't think I can do this."

"You have to, Mel. We have to be prepared."

She didn't want to be prepared. She didn't want to be in this position at all. She wanted to be home with her son worrying about making him do his math homework and getting him to bed on time. Not learning to shoot a gun. Not remembering what Cord's skin felt like against hers. Not feeling so vulnerable and scared and completely out of her element.

"I know how you feel about guns and violence and all of this. But Kane is out there. And like it or not, you might find yourself in a position where you have to use this thing. You have to face reality."

Her chest ached. "A reality I've tried to get away from all my life."

"I know. And I'm sorry."

She wished she could blame it on him. She'd certainly tried. But she knew things weren't as simple as that. As much as she wanted them to be. "It's not your fault. It's Kane's. Now what am I doing wrong?"

He hesitated for a second, then placed his hands on her shoulders and kneaded the muscles. "Just try to gently squeeze. Gentle. Slow. Take in a deep breath and relax your shoulders as you exhale. When you finish breathing out, pull the trigger."

She tried not to moan. His hands on her shoulders felt so good. She couldn't remember when she'd last been touched this way.

Probably the last time Cord had touched her.

Pushing the thoughts from her mind, she raised the gun. She could only think about Ethan. She was doing this for Ethan.

She breathed in, then exhaled in an unsteady stream. She jerked back on the trigger, pulling the gun to the right again. Damn.

He stepped back from her and folded his arms over his chest. "I'm getting in the way. I'll stand back."

She nodded. She needed to concentrate on the gun. On the danger at hand. On protecting Ethan. She pressed her lips into a determined line and raised the gun. Pointing at the lake, she lowered her shoulders and gently squeezed the trigger.

Better. Maybe she was getting somewhere. Maybe she could do this.

"A gun? Cool. Can I learn to shoot?"

Melanie let the gun fall from her hand and clatter to the floor. "Go back to the room, Ethan."

"I just wanted to see what you were doing."

"Back to the room." She didn't want him to see

this. Any of it. "Now, Ethan. I'll be in to explain in a minute."

He stared at her, eyes wide and not understanding. He turned and ran from the room.

"I'll go after him."

Mel grabbed Cord's arm. "No." Tears stung her sinuses and pressed at the backs of her eyes, but she didn't let them fall.

He nodded, as if catching himself. "You're right. I shouldn't go. But do you think you're up to handling it?"

She wasn't up to handling it. Not something this big. Not all alone. What did she know about guns and violence and fear? She'd run away from it. She'd changed her life to avoid it. And she didn't know how to deal with it now. "I tried so hard to keep him away from all this. The guns. The violence."

"I know. And you were right to do that. You raised a great kid."

His words glowed through her, more disconcerting than his touch had been. His sincerity. His concern. The gentle way he'd handled their son when Ethan had cornered him about window washing. It would be easier if Cord didn't care about Ethan. Or if he wasn't good with him. It would be easier if she hadn't seen him make her son smile. "He said he wished you were his father."

Cord jerked his head back as if she'd hit him.

"After you were washing windows together. He said he wanted you around all the time."

He rubbed a hand over his cropped hair. "Maybe the two of you should go out of state. Out of the country, even. Kane couldn't find you then. You'd be safe from him."

It was a good idea, but one that lodged in her chest like a sharp sliver. She forced a nod. "That makes sense."

"We'll talk to McCaskey."

Cord leaned against the wall in his spot next to the elevator and eyed the security panel. Hours had passed since his call to McCaskey. Hours since the SWAT team must have checked out Meredith Unger's house. So where was McCaskey?

Cord needed something to think about. Something besides the fact that Ethan wished Cord was his father. Something besides his need to touch Melanie again. Something besides his idea of sending them far away.

When he'd gotten out of prison, he swore to himself he'd never talk to Mel again. That he'd never intrude on her life. She'd made it clear she wanted nothing to do with him. He figured the least he could do was respect that. But now that Kane had forced the two of them together, now that he knew about his son, the thought of never seeing them again felt like a prison of its own.

The bleat of his cell phone made him jump. He flipped it open and held it to his ear. "Yeah?"

"I'm in the parking lot." McCaskey's voice sounded muffled, strange, despite being so close.

"I'll be down to let you in." Cord disconnected the call and snapped the phone shut. He walked into the area that would eventually become the condo's kitchen and dining room and peered through a bay window at the parking lot below.

Streetlights filtered through maple leaves, casting spotty illumination on a dark-colored sedan. Outside the car stood Reed McCaskey.

As far as Cord could tell, he was alone. But although the distance and darkness prevented him from seeing the expression on the detective's face, Cord got the impression through his rigid posture and movements that something had happened.

And he could bet it was nothing nice.

He turned away from the window and made his way back to the elevator. Stopping at the door, he punched a code into the security panel. The screen flickered to life. The lobby below was empty. The door leading outside locked. Everything seemed as it should be.

Then why the prickle at the back of his neck?

He massaged the sensation away. It had to be the tension that seemed to emanate from Mc-Caskey. Or the strange quality of his voice. Or even Cord's own damn imagination.

He removed the pistol from its holster. There might not be reason to worry, but he wasn't going to take a chance.

"Is he here?" Melanie's voice echoed through the barren hall behind him.

He turned around. "Is Ethan okay?"

She nodded. "I guess I can't be too surprised he was curious about the gun. I mean, all boys are fascinated by guns, right?"

He sure had been. But he doubted Mel would want to hear that right now. "That's what I hear."

She pressed her lips into a slight smile and nodded. "How about Reed? I thought I heard your phone ring."

"I'm going down to let him in." He turned back to the security panel and punched in the code to unlock the elevator.

A low hum rose from the shaft and stopped on their floor. The elevator door slid open.

The stomach-turning sight and strong copper smell sank in slowly, like rain into sodden earth.

Meredith Unger lay on the floor of the elevator, her back propped against the back wall. Her platinum hair was brushed back from her face, the ends tipped in what looked like sticky brown chocolate.

He stared at her hair, trying not to focus on the horror frozen on her face. Or the lifeless shell of her body.

"God help us," Melanie whispered.

Chapter Ten

Red and blue lights pulsed in the darkness outside the condo windows and swirled across bare drywall. Melanie kissed the top of Ethan's head and pulled him close. His hair still smelled like chlorine from the hotel water park, and she inhaled deeply, trying to drag the normalcy of the scent into her lungs. Trying to replace the sweet odor of death that hung in the condo even after the elevator had descended to the lobby.

Cord paced the floor. "I knew she was scared. Maybe I should have gone. Tried to stop the bastard."

"If he was gone by the time the police got there, he would have been gone when you got there, too." She glanced pointedly at Ethan, making sure Cord followed her meaning. "Can we not talk about this?"

"You're right. I didn't think." Staring down at the floor, he resumed pacing.

At least Ethan had been in the bedroom area

when the elevator opened. He hadn't seen Meredith Unger's body. And although she had told him briefly something had happened to explain the presence of the police, she didn't want him to know much more than that. It would only give him nightmares, and he had enough fuel for that fire already.

God knew she'd never erase the image from her mind.

The door to the stairwell opened and Reed McCaskey and Nikki Valducci stepped inside. Crossing the floor toward them, Reed looked from Melanie to Cord and back again. "We need to talk."

Cord narrowed his eyes on the detectives. "I already told you about Meredith Unger's call."

"Not that," Reed said. "I want you to show us the security system."

Nikki's beautiful brown eyes landed on Melanie. "Could you come, too?"

Unease ached deep in Melanie's chest. She couldn't let Ethan out of her sight. Not now. It wasn't that he was upset, he didn't seem to be anything other than curious about what was going on. She was a different story. She needed to be close for her own sake. Her own sense of security. "Can you play the Game Boy with your headphones again?"

"Mom...why can't I hear what's going on?"

She touched his cheek, still baby soft yet starting to take on the leaner look of a teenager. So grown-up, yet still a little boy. "You're going to have to trust me on this, honey. Okay?"

He picked up the game, plugged in the headphones and slipped them on his head. A flick of a switch, and his thumbs were hitting the buttons with record speed.

She kissed his forehead, and for once he didn't wipe it off. Climbing to her feet, she focused on Reed McCaskey. "The other end of the room is as far as I'm going."

"That should work." He led them to the spot she was standing when she saw Meredith Unger's body.

The air seemed heavier here. And even though the elevator car and body were now several floors below, she could swear a sense of horror clung to the walls and lingered like that unmistakable odor.

"How are you holding up?" Nikki asked.

Not a question she wanted to think too much about. "Okay, I guess. How did he find us?"

"We're trying to determine that." Reed focused on Cord. "Is there a security camera showing the parking lot?"

Cord shook his head. "Just the lobby entrance and the garage."

"Where are the tapes kept?"

"It's digital. The cameras are activated by motion sensors."

"How long are the images kept?"

"They should be there until the hard drive is full. Then the oldest images are erased. Have you talked to the builder?"

Reed shook his head. "We will tomorrow. We want to keep this as quiet as we can until we can get the three of you to a safe place. Do you know how to access what those cameras recorded?"

"You can view them from the panel." Cord strode to the elevator, Reed, Nikki and Melanie following in his wake.

He punched in the code, and the image of the garage filled the small screen. Cord's truck sat alone among dust and the hulking shapes of construction equipment. "I'll just set it back—"

The image flickered and Cord's truck was suddenly just entering the garage.

The door to the stairwell opened and Detective Stan Perreth barged into the corridor. His face looked pasty, as if he was ill. Chewing on an unlit cigarette, he joined them at the security panel without saying a word. The scent of cigarette smoke hung in the air around him.

On the monitor, Cord's truck came to a halt and the driver's door swung open. A man stepped out of the truck and glanced up at the camera. His dyed red hair glowed in the garage's dim light.

"Kane." His name burst from Melanie's lips.

But this was wrong. All wrong. "Why is he driving your truck?"

Cord let out a breath but said nothing. The detectives remained silent, as if everyone was holding their collective breath, waiting to see what happened next.

On the screen, Kane circled to the back of the truck. He opened the window of the topper and the tail gate. Reaching inside, he pulled out a large object cloaked in black plastic. She didn't have to see through it to know what was inside.

Meredith Unger.

Hefting his burden to his shoulder, Kane carried it to the elevator. After waiting a few seconds for the doors to open, he disappeared inside.

"You punk-ass bastard." Perreth's voice growled low and dangerous. "You lent Daddy your truck?"

Cord shook his head.

Melanie narrowed her eyes on Perreth. Kane had used Cord's truck. The evidence was right there on the screen. But it didn't make sense. There had to be an explanation. Cord didn't *give* his truck to Kane. She'd stake her life on that.

Come to think of it, she was. "Is there more on the recording?"

Cord was already reaching for the panel. He touched a few buttons, and an earlier image came to life on the screen.

The elevator door in the garage slid open and Kane stepped out. He walked to the truck. He looked relaxed, as if he didn't have a care in the world.

Melanie focused on the digital time-readout in the lower-right-hand corner of the screen. "That was this morning."

Reed nodded. "Sure enough."

On the security screen, Kane climbed into the truck. Using a knife, he dug at the steering column of Cord's truck. A minute later the engine jumped to life, exhaust puffing out the tailpipe. He backed up and drove the truck out of the garage.

"That still doesn't show how he got in the building to begin with," Nikki said.

"I'll go back further." Cord punched a few buttons.

The image of the garage flickered to the screen for the third time. The parking space next to the elevator was again empty. Cord's truck nosed onto the screen just as it had in the first image they'd seen.

This time Cord sat in the driver's seat, his shoulders wider than Kane's. And beside him in the truck were two smaller shadows. Her and Ethan. "Are you sure there's not another one? That's when we first arrived."

"This is it," Cord said.

On the screen Cord parked the truck, and the three of them climbed out. After loading up with supplies, they disappeared into the elevator.

"That tells us nothing." Detective Perreth growled.

Reed held up a hand. "Wait."

Seconds ticked by. Silence hung heavy in the room. Not even the beeps of Ethan's game were audible. Suddenly the window of the truck topper lurched. A hand emerged from the truck bed and pushed it open.

Dryden Kane climbed out into the garage.

Melanie couldn't believe what she was seeing. Panic crashed over her. Her stomach felt sick. "He was in the truck with us? He was here all the time?" She looked up at Cord, hoping for disagreement and explanation, anything that would make what she'd just seen on the security screen not true.

His lips flattened into a bloodless line.

Melanie's throat closed. Of course he didn't have an explanation. There was no explanation to give. Kane had been in the truck with them. He'd been in the building. Neither of them had had a clue.

And if Kane could get that close to them without their knowledge, what chance did they really have of getting out of this situation alive?

CORD STARED AT THE PICKUP on the screen, his gut twisting into a hard knot. Kane had been there all along, hidden under the jumble of window-washing drop cloths and buckets in the back of his truck. If not for the locks on the elevator and stairwell, he could have waltzed right into the penthouse anytime he wanted.

Melanie searched his face as if waiting for an answer. An answer he couldn't give.

Finally she glanced at the detectives. "I have to go. Ethan needs me." Melanie left the entry hall and crossed the great room to the spot where Ethan sat, still fully immersed in his game. The boy didn't need Mel, not right this moment. It was the other way around. Melanie needed her son close. She needed to touch him and make sure he was safe.

Cord couldn't blame her. Watching her lower herself to the floor next to him and circle her arm around his shoulders, Cord wished he could join them.

Instead he focused on McCaskey. "Melanie and Ethan need to get out of here."

"I can find a safe location. Same arrangement as before."

"No. Not like before."

McCaskey narrowed his eyes. "What do you have in mind?"

"I want them on a plane. Under assumed names."

"Wait a second." Nikki Valducci waved her hands in front of her. "You can't do that."

"Why the hell not?"

"Kane has decided you are to put this reception

together. He wants you to go to the florist, to the bakery. He's pegged *you* as his contact."

"So?"

"He thinks you might be sympathetic to him, that he might be able to manipulate you the way he did Louis Ingersoll."

Cord had seen everything he needed to know about Louis Ingersoll on the nonstop television coverage a couple of months ago. Also known as the Copycat Killer, Ingersoll had carried out crimes identical to Kane's while the elder serial killer was behind bars. About the last person he aspired to be was Louis Ingersoll. Or Kane. "So he's chosen me. What does that have to do with sending Mel and Ethan somewhere safe?"

"You said Kane mentioned Ethan serving the cake. Sending him away is going to tip Kane off. It's going to take away what he sees as your vulnerable spot."

"That's the idea."

She shook her head. "He's not going to trust you if that happens. He's got to believe he can control you."

"So you want to do what? Use Ethan as bait for some damn trap of yours?"

"Not him," Nikki said. "Of course not. I just don't want to tip Kane off. If he feels he controls you, he'll be more likely to make a mistake."

"I agree there's a place for proactive techniques," McCaskey said. "But a child will not be involved. You have my word on that, Turner."

"But you do agree? About using Kane's wedding reception to set a trap?" Nikki shifted her boots on the plywood floor, as if she couldn't keep still.

She had been pushing to set a trap for Kane since the second time Cord had laid eyes on her. Now that Kane had set the table, she was ready to serve dinner.

A thought that made Cord more than a little uneasy. "So if not Ethan, who *are* you planning to serve up as bait?"

"The person he really wants. The person he almost killed before." She eyed McCaskey.

"You just lost me, Nikki," he said.

"But, Reed, you know that's the only way a trap will work. He wants Diana. He'll risk a lot to get her."

"I'm not talking about this again."

"You could at least tell Diana what's going on, let her make up her own mind."

McCaskey glowered.

"Time to put up or shut up, McCaskey." Detective Perreth flicked his cigarette lighter to life and touched it to the cigarette in his mouth.

McCaskey turned to Perreth. "Put that out."

"It's a private residence. There aren't any smoking laws about that. Yet, anyway."

"Kane is showing signs of stress." Nikki's face grew more animated. From the look of things, she was just warming up. "Being on the run, the media coverage, the killing, it all adds up. Soon he'll start getting sloppy, acting on instinct instead of planning. Eventually even psychopaths like Kane make mistakes. It's the perfect time to trap him with his own game. If we give him something he feels is worth taking some risks for, he'll take them."

Nikki might have the education to back her up, but Cord wasn't sure he agreed with her theory. "What makes you think he feels stress? He seemed pretty cool carrying Meredith Unger's body in here tonight. And when he tried to take Ethan in the hotel, he was cold." He'd seen it before in the pen. Killers so cold-blooded you'd swear they didn't have a heart in their bodies. But none of them could have held a candle to what he'd seen in Kane.

"He seems that way, but he's not killing the way he likes to kill anymore. He's not hunting. He's not torturing. He likes to take his time. He likes to hear the women scream, taste their fear. That's what turns him on."

"So he didn't have time. He had to figure I called you. That you were on your way to Meredith Unger's house. Lack of time doesn't equal stress."

"I don't think it's that simple."

McCaskey's frown deepened. "You think he's desperate. Desperate to kill Diana."

Nikki nodded. "He has always fixated on a woman in the past. First his wife, Adrianna. Then Risa Madsen. He killed women who looked like the one he was obsessed with until he worked up the excitement to kill the woman herself. After what happened at Banesbridge with Diana, I can't see him letting that go until she's dead. And likely Sylvie, too."

"The family. That's what Meredith Unger said when she called, that Kane wanted to be reunited with his family."

Nikki nodded, as if not surprised. "Killing his daughters and transforming his son and grandson into versions of himself. He risked a lot showing up at that hotel. He risked a lot coming here. I'm sure if he had any idea where Diana and Sylvie were, he'd stop at nothing. We have to use that to catch him."

"I'm not using anyone for bait." McCaskey focused on Nikki. "You've put in a lot of time studying serial killers, but you still have no real idea what Kane is capable of. I do. I'm not taking chances I don't have to take."

Nikki shot him a look as if to say the debate wasn't over.

"So what happens now?" Cord asked.

"I'll take the three of you somewhere safe for the night."

"And Mel and Ethan? What about getting them out of town?"

McCaskey gave him a nod. "That sounds like a good idea. Give me a destination, and we'll get them to the airport tomorrow. And in the meantime, we'll figure out what to do about Kane."

Cord let out a breath but he didn't relax. He wouldn't until that plane was off the ground and Melanie and Ethan were on their way to some far-off place where Kane couldn't reach them.

And neither could he.

JANET BLANKENSHIP couldn't believe her luck. Swinging her BMW to the curb on Gorham Street and straight into a vacant parking space just around the corner from State Street, she let a wide smile spread over her lips.

Tonight was definitely her night. Not only had Adam gotten his hands on tickets for the sold-out production of *Wicked* at the Overture Center, but the Pilates class was really starting to pay off. As evidenced by how incredible she looked in her new Alberta Ferretti cocktail dress.

She slipped on her prized pair of Jimmy Choo slides with heels so high she couldn't drive in them and took one last look in the visor's vanity mirror.

The movers and shakers in Madison wouldn't know what hit them.

She started to open the door when a shadow appeared outside. The door tore from her grasp. A hand shot into the car and grabbed her by the hair.

It had to be some kind of mistake. Some kind of joke. "What do you think you're doing?"

Ice-blue eyes focused on her. Thin lips pulled back from white teeth in a chilling smile.

Fear cut through disbelief. She opened her mouth to call for help, to scream.

"Shut up." His other hand came up. A knife gleamed dully in the streetlight. "Unless you want me to cut out your voice box. Might be fun."

This couldn't be happening. Not just yards away from a busy street. Not to her. "Take the car. Go ahead. I won't tell anyone."

Using her hair for leverage, the man shoved her over the center console and climbed into the driver's seat. He slammed the soundproof door closed.

She tried to breathe, to think. Her chest felt as if it was being crushed, as if she couldn't get enough air. "Take the car. It's worth a lot of money. And my purse." She shoved her black Prada handbag at him.

Those eyes drilled into her, cold and sharp. The

cool mint of his breath fanned her face. "I want more than your car."

"My husband will pay you. He's a respected eye surgeon. He'll give you anything you want. Please. You can't do this. You don't realize who I am."

"Yes I do."

She dragged in a breath, the air still not coming easy, but at least it came. "Then you know. You know what my husband can do for you. You know he'll pay."

"But I don't want him to pay."

"What do you want? Anything. I can get it for you."

He brought the knife up, under her chin. Tracing the blade's tip down her chest, he stopped at the vee neck of her dress. "I don't want your husband to pay. I want you to pay."

Panic congealed in her veins. She couldn't move. She just stared at the knife nestled in her cleavage.

He brought the blade down. The black silk gave way. The light tearing sound ripped through her ears like a scream. Tears rose in her eyes, blurring his face. He reached the hem. Her dress gaped open.

"You can't do this." Her voice hitched and trembled.

He fitted the blade between the cups of her bra. The fabric slit under sharp steel and fell away. He moved to her pantyhose.

"I thought you said you know who I am, what I can do for you." A sob worked up her throat and choked her.

"I do know who you are. I know better than you do." He stared at her naked body with dead eyes. No arousal. No emotion. He raised the knife to the notch in her collar bone. "You're nothing."

Chapter Eleven

Cord, Mel and Ethan had their essential belongings packed and ready to go in less than five minutes. They followed McCaskey into the stairwell and descended the five stories to the garage level.

"You're going to have to leave your truck," McCaskey said, shoving open the garage door.

Cord let Mel and Ethan step into the garage first, then spared his truck a glance. "When will I get it back?"

"Not sure. The techs will need to go over every inch."

Great. So much for the window-washing business. Not that there was anything left even if he had the truck. The builder would be upset enough to learn he was camping out in his luxury condos. Cord was sure he'd be extra thrilled now that the property was the scene of a serial killer's "display." He'd be willing to bet *that* would put a crimp in the upscale condo market. "Just get us some-where safe."

McCaskey led them to an unmarked sedan parked near the garage's door. Mel and Ethan climbed in the back, and Cord took the front passenger seat. McCaskey climbed behind the wheel and started the engine. "Sit low in your seats. If Kane is out there waiting, we don't want to give him an easy target to follow."

Mel and Ethan disappeared behind Cord's seat. Folding his legs against the dash, Cord slid as low as he could manage.

McCaskey gave one of the cops in the garage a signal. The garage door lifted, and they drove out into the night.

Bands of illumination from streetlights moved through the car in stripes. The hum of the engine blended with the whisper of tires on pavement.

McCaskey stopped and started, negotiating stop signs and lights. Finally they blended with the flow of traffic on East Johnson Street. "You can sit up."

Cord unfolded his body. He glanced around, noting the swarm of headlights shining through windows and in the rearview mirror. Any one of those cars could have Kane behind the wheel. He could be hanging back, watching, following, and they'd never know. He'd be just another set of headlights in the flow of weekend traffic.

In the backseat, Melanie and Ethan sat up and looked around. "Where are we going?" Mel asked.

"We need to talk about our next move. We're going to meet with Diana and Sylvie."

"So you are considering Nikki's plan?"

A pained look flashed across McCaskey's face. "A version of it. Maybe."

"Why did you let her believe you weren't?"

"Perreth was there."

"Perreth?" The detective was a dick, but… "You like Perreth for the police department leak?"

"Let's just say I found something at Meredith Unger's house that makes me wonder."

"What?" Mel asked from the backseat.

"Phone messages he left."

Interesting. Cord wanted to know more. "About Kane?"

"About trying to get a date. Seems Meredith wasn't returning his calls."

"That doesn't mean he's the leak," Mel said.

"No. But it does mean I'm not going to take a chance by letting him know what I'm planning."

"What are you planning exactly?"

"We'll talk about it later. Nikki was right about one thing. If I don't include Diana in this discussion, I might as well turn in my wedding ring right now. I learned that the hard way." His lips turned up at the corners, a mixture of annoyance and pride. "We have more important things to figure out before we get there."

"Like what?" Still clutching Ethan's hand, Mel leaned forward in her seat.

"Like where you and Ethan want to go."

Mel's eyebrows rose. She looked to Cord for an explanation.

"I talked to McCaskey about getting the two of you some plane tickets." Just saying it made his chest tighten. After tomorrow, he would never see Mel and Ethan again. He'd put them on a plane and watch them fly out of his life. And when they returned to Wisconsin, he'd be gone.

Mel held his gaze for a moment, as if she was envisioning the future, too. But as much as Cord would like to think her warm brown eyes were filled with regret, he knew that was probably not the case. More likely she felt relieved.

She looked away from him and down at their son. "What do you think, Ethan? Should we go to Disney World?"

"Could we?"

"I don't know why not." She looked up at McCaskey. "I'll give you my credit card if you make the arrangements."

The detective gave her a nod in the rearview mirror.

She smiled at their son. Hands down one of the

most beautiful things Cord had ever seen. "Disney World it is."

"Cool. Is Cord going, too?"

Ethan's question plunged into his gut and twisted like a Christmas tree shank. He waited for Mel to answer.

She hesitated. "No, honey. He can't."

He peered over the seat at his son and swallowed into an aching throat. "I can't make it. I have to work."

He dropped his gaze to his hand cradled in his mother's. "Oh."

Cord peered out the window again, trying to focus on anything but the disappointment in his son's voice. And the disappointment lodged in his own chest.

The headlights behind them thinned as they traveled farther away from the heart of the isthmus. One car turned off toward the interstate. Another veered into a neighborhood. They arched north around the curve of Lake Mendota, the opposite shore to the isthmus where the city lights stretched. Soon only dark highway twisted ahead.

And one car still followed behind.

"Do you see that?" Cord said to McCaskey, careful to keep his voice too low for Mel and Ethan to hear.

McCaskey glanced in the rearview mirror and

nodded. Judging from his reaction, he not only spotted the car, he'd been watching it. "It's been with us since we got on East Johnson. I'm going to call in the plate."

MELANIE'S HEART JUMPED at the intensity ringing in Cord's and Reed's voices. She might not be able to hear what they were saying, but she didn't have to. Something was going on.

She tightened her grip on Ethan's hand.

"What's wrong, Mom?"

"Nothing, honey. I'm just tired." She plastered a smile to her lips. She hadn't meant to show her tension to Ethan. She didn't want to upset him. God knew he'd been through enough. "Are you looking forward to Disney?"

"I guess."

"What do you want to do first? Epcot Center or the Magic Kingdom?"

He glanced up at the front seat. "Is somebody following us?"

So much for her sunny act. She let the false smile fall from her lips and wrapped an arm around Ethan's shoulder, pulling him close. "I don't know."

Reed held his radio to his mouth and talked in a low voice.

Melanie reached into the front seat and touched Cord's shoulder.

Cord looked back over the seat. Shadows cupped the edges of his face, settling into the fine lines beginning to fan out around his eyes.

Strange, just a day ago, she'd thought the dashboard glow and shadows made him look hard. Now she could see the man under the thick shell he'd grown. The shell of tattoos and muscle. "What's going on?"

"McCaskey's calling in the license plate of the car behind us. He's just making sure it's nothing to worry about."

She let herself fall back against the seat. Cord was probably right. It was probably nothing. At least she would hold onto that hope.

The buzz of a voice sounded in the front seat, but she couldn't make out the words.

Reed said a few more unintelligible things into the radio, then glanced at Melanie in the rearview mirror. "The car is registered to a woman named Janet Blankenship."

The name held no significance for her. She waited for him to go on.

He returned the radio to the dash. "She lives in the general area. Over toward Middleton. Probably on her way home. You might as well relax."

Melanie wanted to relax, God knew. But she doubted she could. Not until she knew her son was safe. At least for the night.

Reed swung the car onto a remote road flanked on both sides by forest. Behind them, the car whizzed by on the highway, going west toward Middleton.

She let out a breath. Thank God.

Reed accelerated through oak forest and down a winding road. A half mile down, the forest thinned. Lake Mendota opened up alongside the road. Across the black waves, the city lights twinkled. The capitol dome glowed like a tiny white beacon. Melanie narrowed her eyes on the road ahead, trying to see through the darkness. "Where are they staying out here?"

"You'll see."

Mailboxes dotted the shoulder of the road ahead. Houses too large for their lots crowded shoulder-to-shoulder along the shore.

She tried to stifle the unease shifting inside her. It didn't seem very secure. Not as secure as the condo downtown. But she couldn't believe Reed would leave his wife's safety to chance. Would he?

She turned around and peered out the back window at the darkness. No one following. She let her gaze linger over Ethan. He stared out the window at the houses. He looked so tired, as tired as she felt. It would be good to get away. To have some fun. To fill his eyes once again with that shining joy.

The joy she'd seen when he was washing windows with Cord.

She turned back around and focused on the road ahead. The line of houses ended and the shoreline opened into a park. Swing sets and jungle gyms etched dark against the sparkle of waves kicked up by stiff wind. A long pier jutted into the water. A large boat bobbed at the end.

Reed pulled into the parking lot.

"The boat? They're on the boat?" she asked.

"A boat on the lake. Can't get much more secure than that." Cord nodded with approval.

They climbed from the car. Next to her, Ethan's eyes grew wide. "We get to go on it?"

Reed nodded. "Yup. You're going to sleep on the boat tonight."

"Cool."

Melanie let a smile surface to her lips. Maybe things were looking up. A night on a boat. A plane ride to Disney World. Days of fun in the Magic Kingdom. Maybe it was just what they needed to leave the trauma of the past few days behind and go on with their lives.

Lives of which Cord couldn't be a part.

After loading down with sleeping bags and duffel bags, they stepped onto the pier. Wind whipped at Melanie's face, lashing her hair across her cheeks and into her eyes.

"Here. Let me take that." Cord lifted her bag from her shoulder, freeing one hand to hold the hair out of her face.

She wasn't used to getting help. Not from anyone. She was used to doing things on her own. But right now, with all that had happened the past few days, she appreciated the gesture far more than she should. "Thanks."

"No problem."

She looked ahead, focusing on the boat. On Ethan. On anything but Cord. They continued down the long pier. The boat loomed large in front of them. It had to be one of the biggest she'd ever seen on Lake Mendota. A boat more suited to Lake Michigan or trolling along one of the coasts.

The shadow of a man appeared on the deck, a small rifle in his hands.

"It's us, Bryce. Ethan, do you want to go first?" Reed motioned to a ladder on the back of the boat. Holding out a hand, he helped Ethan step from the pier to the ladder.

Melanie tried to keep her pulse from jumping at the sight of the weapon. Soon this would be over. Soon she would have Ethan far away from guns and violence. Soon he'd return to a carefree, fun-loving boy again.

A boy without a dad.

"Melanie?" Reed helped her to the ladder.

Gripping the cold rungs, she climbed to the boat's deck behind Ethan. Cord followed, then Reed. Once all of them were aboard, Bryce and his weapon disappeared to the front of the boat. The engine rumbled to life, its low grind vibrating through the vessel. The boat pulled away from the pier and headed out on black waves.

"Where are Diana and Sylvie?" Cord asked.

Reed gestured to a narrow staircase leading to the boat's lower level. "Go ahead."

Melanie started down the stairs, Ethan behind her. It was warmer down here away from the whipping wind. But without the pier or land or distant lights to judge the boat's movement by, she felt dizzy and unsure, as if the steps would fall out from under her at any moment. She gripped the railing to keep some sense of balance.

A warm light shone on wood paneling below. Although the boat looked huge from the outside, everything seemed tiny inside. A miniature kitchen opened at the base of the stairs. Two small cabins flanked the kitchen, one on either side. She headed for the cabin that glowed with warm light. Stepping inside, she met two sets of familiar light blue eyes.

One of the blond twins jumped to her feet. "You must be Melanie. I'm Diana."

The other blonde remained seated, one hand cradling a slightly bulging belly. A diamond eyebrow ring sparkled in the light. "Sylvie, here."

Cord's sisters. Melanie offered a genuine smile. "Melanie. It's great to finally meet you."

"It's great meeting you, too. I haven't even met my brother yet." Sylvie smiled, though she looked a little green. Whether from seasickness or pregnancy, Melanie couldn't tell.

After Cord and Reed joined them and they finished the round of introductions, Diana gave Reed a kiss and they all carved out spots in the cramped little cabin.

Diana smiled at Ethan. "Would you like to watch a DVD? We have a bunch in the other cabin."

Ethan jumped at the chance. And as much as Melanie wanted him close enough to touch, she knew from the exhausted look in his eyes that the TV suggestion was a good one. She left him splayed on the bed in the other cabin watching a superhero movie and returned to find Cord talking quietly with his sisters.

For a moment she just stood in the doorway and stared. They looked so much alike, the eyes, the cheekbones, that for a moment she couldn't breathe. She'd never thought of Cord having a family before. She'd known his mother, but there had been no connection between her and Cord. She had acted as if he was an intruder in her life, someone she didn't trust, let alone care about.

But just seeing the way Diana smiled at him and the way Sylvie tilted her head as she listened—really listened—to what he had to say, made her realize for the first time that Cord had his own life beyond her. That he had his own roots. His own family. Even if he was only just starting to know them.

"Take a seat, Melanie. Everyone. We have some things to discuss." Reed's voice cut through the small talk with the harsh tone of reality.

Melanie sank into a chair at the edge of the cabin, Cord next to her. Diana and Sylvie perched on the edge of the bed. It wasn't until Bryce's footsteps clunked down the stairs and he entered the room that Melanie realized the boat had stopped moving forward. With the roll of the waves, they were bobbing up and down so much, she hadn't been able to tell.

In a low voice, Reed filled them in on Meredith Unger's murder and her call to Cord. He brushed over Nikki Valducci's arguments for setting a trap, but no matter how much he downplayed his fellow detective's ideas, Melanie could see the determination harden in Diana's eyes, just as it had in Cord's.

Diana brushed a lock of blond hair over one shoulder. "We need to give him his wedding reception."

Reed closed his eyes for a moment. Opening them, he sank down onto the bed next to his wife and took her hand in his. "We can't do that."

"Why not? Cord and I can pull it off. Sylvie can stay here."

Sylvie opened her mouth to protest, but Diana held up a hand to cut her off. "You have to think of the baby, Syl. You can stay with Melanie and Ethan."

Sylvie reluctantly agreed.

Diana closed her hand over Reed's. "Cord can deliver me to Kane. And you'll be right behind him."

"You really want to do that?" The horror in Bryce Walker's voice echoed the feeling in Melanie's own stomach.

"No. Of course not." Diana shifted on the bed, no doubt uncomfortable just thinking about the prospect. "I still have nightmares about him. But those nightmares aren't just going to disappear. Especially with him free."

Reed shook his head. "There has to be another way."

"What if there isn't?" Diana said.

"Why don't I go alone?"

All eyes focused on Cord. Worry dug into the back of Melanie's neck. "You can't go alone."

"Why not? I could have a couple of dummies in the car, or better, cops. By the time Kane figures out they aren't Diana and Sylvie, he'll have a gun muzzle pointed at his head."

Melanie shook her head. "It's too dangerous."

"How is it less dangerous to have Diana with me?"

She shook her head again. That wasn't what she was getting at. "Meeting with him at all is too dangerous. This trap is too dangerous."

"I agree."

Melanie gave Reed a nod, glad to have the detective on her side.

"But if Cord is willing, we could set up a cop to act as Diana," Reed added.

So much for an ally. Reed McCaskey was willing to put Cord's life on the line. As long as his wife was safe, he didn't see the problem. "And you're going to put Cord into the middle of this unarmed?"

Reed pressed his lips into a line.

She looked to Cord. Neither one seemed to want to answer that one. Not a big surprise considering the gun and pep talk Reed had given Cord after Kane had tried to kidnap Ethan.

"And if you kill him, Cord, what happens then? Do you go back to prison?" She spun to Reed. The detective might have good reason for wanting

Kane dead. Heck, the world had good reason. But if Cord was the one who pulled that trigger or slipped a knife between the monster's ribs, what would happen to him?

"I can't promise anything. I have to uphold the law."

"So you can suggest Cord kill a man, even give him a weapon, and then you dust off your hands and walk away?"

"It's not like that, Melanie."

"It's not going to work anyway," Diana said, cutting off her husband.

"Why not?"

"Kane won't fall for it. He's smart. He's going to be looking for something like that."

"Not if he's desperate enough to get his hands on you."

"Even then. I'm telling you, you're underestimating him."

"As Nikki said, he's showing signs of stress. And he's desperate." Reed's tone was firm, no doubt meant to cut off debate. "It's settled. Tomorrow we'll take Melanie and Ethan to the airport, then Cord can pick up Kane's flowers and cake. And we'll take it from there."

Melanie shook her head. She didn't like it. Not that she had any say as to what Cord decided, but almost wished she did. She wished she could demand he come to Disney. She wished she could demand he stay as far from Dryden Kane as possible.

"I'm not setting out to murder him. Believe me, Mel. But I am going to protect myself. I am going to protect my family."

My family. Ethan, Diana and Sylvie. They were all Cord's family.

The same sensation she'd felt after she'd set Ethan up with his DVD swept over her. The feeling that Cord was connected. If she thought about it, he was more connected than she was.

"Your son is so lucky, Melanie."

Melanie turned to look at Sylvie. "Lucky?"

"I know we just met. But even in these few minutes, I can tell Ethan has quite a mother in you. And a brave, selfless father in Cord. One who really cares about him." Her lips tilted upward in a sad smile. "Neither Diana nor I have ever known that."

"Mom?"

Ice filled Melanie's veins. She turned toward the cabin's doorway and met her son's wide eyes.

"Is Cord my dad?"

Chapter Twelve

Numbness settled into Melanie's bones. There had to be words to explain, words that would take the look of betrayal from her son's eyes. But if those words did exist, she had no idea what they were. "I'm sorry, Ethan. I should have told you."

Tears rushed into his eyes. He spun around and ran out of the room. On the other side of the galley kitchen, a door slammed.

"I'm so sorry," Sylvie said in a horrified whisper. "I thought he was in the other room. I had no idea—"

Melanie held up a hand. She couldn't stand to hear Sylvie's apologies. Not for something *she* had done. Good reasons or not, she had lied to her son. And even after he'd confessed his wish that Cord was his father, she still hadn't come clean. "It's not your fault, Sylvie. It's mine. If you'll all excuse me, I have to talk to him."

Cord grasped her arm before she could make it out the door. He looked down at her with hurting eyes. Lost eyes. She could tell by his look that he wanted to help, wanted her to tell him what to do.

She couldn't manage. Not now. She didn't have any idea what to do herself. She just needed to be with her son. To touch him. To tell him she loved him. To make sure he was going to be okay.

To make sure he forgave her. "I'll be back. I just need to see him first. Alone."

Cord nodded and released her arm.

She hurried out the door and through the kitchen. The boat swayed under her feet, making her feel more shaky, more uncertain. All her life she'd wanted to protect Ethan. How could she have failed so miserably? She rapped on the door and pushed it open.

Ethan sat on the edge of the bed, his back to her. He held his shoulders stiff, as if he could force the tears back or the screams or whatever he must want to do.

"Ethan?"

He didn't move.

She closed the door behind her and stepped into the room. "Can we talk?"

He shook his head.

"I want to try to explain things to you. I want to help you understand."

He said nothing, his silence cutting deeper than vicious words ever could.

She opened her mouth, then closed it without saying anything. What could she say? She could never explain why she'd lied about his father, why she'd told him Cord was dead. The most eloquent words on earth would never make him understand.

Sylvie was right. Having parents who cared was a priceless thing. More important than all the money or opportunity or luck in the world. And Cord cared. He cared now, and he would have cared when he was eighteen. Would have, if she'd told him the truth.

And that was exactly why she hadn't. Because she'd known he would want to be part of his son's life. Because she'd known she would want him to be part. Because she didn't want Ethan to live through what she had. What so many of the kids in her neighborhood had. The humiliation of a father in prison. The blow to his self-esteem. The tendency to follow in the path of parents.

The path it had taken all her strength and determination to escape.

But she couldn't explain all that. Not that Ethan would listen now if she tried. The best she could do was apologize. If he knew how bad she felt, maybe in time he'd forgive her. Maybe then she could make him understand. "I'm sorry, Ethan. What I did wasn't right. I should have told you the truth about your dad from the beginning. I should have told you both."

Her son's shoulders rose and fell with each breath, but he didn't turn around. He didn't say a word.

Tears slid over her cheeks and tainted her lips with salt. She couldn't do this alone. She had for ten years, but she couldn't do it anymore. She'd made a mistake. A horrible mistake.

And she had no idea how she was going to fix it.

CORD STARED at the closed door of the cabin. The boat was quiet, once again anchored in some remote location in the lake. They'd dropped Diana off with McCaskey at the pier, a chance for husband and wife to be together before returning the next day. Though judging from his sister's determination, he'd bet they'd spend the night arguing about how to trap Kane.

Sylvie and Walker had finally gone to bed, closing themselves in the other cabin. Cord had tried to make Sylvie feel better, but he doubted his efforts had worked. Her comments had been meant as praise. She'd had no idea her simple observation had been a time bomb in disguise.

The door to Ethan and Melanie's cabin rattled and the knob turned. Melanie stepped out into the narrow kitchen. Puffy lower lids and bloodshot eyes told him she'd spent a good portion of the time in the cabin crying.

He reached out and touched her arm, unsure how to let her know he was here for her, that he wanted to help.

"I'm all right."

She didn't look anywhere near "all right." "Ethan?"

"He's angry. Confused."

"What did he say?"

"He wouldn't talk to me."

"The whole time you were in there?"

She shook her head. Tears sparkled in the corners of her eyes. Her chest heaved, then lowered with a jerky motion. "You know, they say it's painful when your child lets you down. It's not. It's much worse the other way around."

She was beating herself up. Taking the responsibility for everything on her shoulders. Taking the blame. "You did the right thing. The only thing you could do. You couldn't tell him."

"He doesn't see it that way." She let out a long breath. "I'm not sure if I see it that way anymore, either."

He shook his head. An ache throbbed deep in his throat. He didn't understand what she was saying. He wasn't sure he wanted to. "He'll get over it."

"Did you?"

"Me?"

"Your mother didn't tell you who your father was."

"Seeing that he's a serial killer, I think that was the least of her sins." He caught himself. His bitterness toward his mother wasn't helping. And it had nothing to do with Melanie's relationship with Ethan. "Scratch that. I don't have much to say about my mother. At least, nothing nice. But you're not like her. Don't you even think that for a second."

She pressed her lips together as if she'd made up her mind not to listen.

Cord took her hands in his. Her skin was soft yet cold. "You knew my mother. You knew what she was like. She expected me to be a bad kid from the time I was born. Expected me to lie, to steal. I think she was actually relieved when I killed Snake. I think to her it was proof that she'd had me figured out all along."

"Because she expected you to grow up like your father. Like Dryden Kane."

Time for *him* to take responsibility. "I did."

"No, you didn't."

"I killed a man."

"In self-defense. That's not the same as a man who kills more than a dozen women for enjoyment. A man who tortures and humiliates. A man who kills anyone who gets in the way."

"Maybe not, but I landed in prison, just like my mother always said I would."

"I'm sorry you had to go through that."

So was he. He was sorry for all of it. The mistakes that were his fault and the mistakes that weren't. "The thing is, you aren't like her. You've always thought the best of Ethan. You've always *done* the best for him. He's a smart kid. He'll see that. He'll know."

"God, I hope so. Right now I'll be happy if he ever talks to me again."

He ran his fingers over her hands, drinking in the fine lines of her bones under her skin. So delicate. So fragile. "You were right not to tell him, Mel. About me or about Kane. Let it go."

She closed her eyes. "Dryden Kane. I didn't even think about him. I wonder if Ethan has."

Oh, hell. As if swallowing the fact that his father was an ex-con wasn't enough for one night, the kid also had to choke down the idea that his grandfather was a serial killer.

"I don't know what to do. For the first time in my life, I have no idea." She looked down at the floor. Taking a deep breath, she returned her gaze to his face. "Help me."

He couldn't have heard her right. "Mel?"

"Go in there with me. Help me talk to him. No matter what has happened in the past, you're his father, Cord. He needs you now."

As she looked into his eyes, the void in his chest started filling. With strength. With hope. With purpose. He didn't know if he could do this. Didn't know if he'd be any good at all. But he couldn't say no. One look in Mel's eyes, one thought of his son behind that door, and he knew refusal wasn't possible. "You'll have to show me how."

MELANIE FOLLOWED Cord back into the cabin. The room was dark, only the light streaming in from the kitchen breaking the shadow and glistening in Ethan's hair. He sat with his back stiff, just as he'd been when she left him. A kid dealing with problems no adult should have to face.

The press of tears stung her sinuses. Her arms ached to wrap around her son, to take away his hurt. But it hadn't worked before and it wouldn't work now. She could only hope that Cord's presence would make a difference. That he would be able to talk to Ethan where she had failed.

"Hey, Ethan," Cord said.

Ethan stared down at his hands folded between his knees, as if he hadn't heard a thing.

Cord stepped toward the bed, then hesitated. He glanced back at Melanie.

She gestured to the bed with a nod.

He stepped around the bed. "Mind if I sit down?"

Ethan looked up at him. His eyes glowed in the darkness. Shadows cupped his pale cheeks, making them look almost as round as they'd been when he was a baby. He looked back down to his hands.

Melanie let a breath escape. At least he didn't object.

Cord slid between Ethan's knees and the wall and sank to the bed. Melanie sat on Ethan's other side. "I know you're angry with me, Ethan. But we need to talk."

He looked away, as if too disgusted to look at her. "I'm tired."

She tried to grab hold of the ache in her chest, to keep it from overwhelming her. "I thought I was doing the right thing, not telling you about Cord. But I made a mistake. I'm sorry for that."

Ethan didn't look at her, didn't acknowledge that she'd said a word. He looked up at Cord. "Didn't you want me? Is that why Mom lied?"

"Cord didn't know about you, Ethan. I didn't tell him."

His head whipped around. His eyes cut into her like lasers. "Why?"

"Because I was afraid." She swallowed back the tears. She couldn't break down. Ethan was right to be angry with her, and she had to be strong enough to take it.

"We grew up in a really bad place with a lot of bad people," Cord said in an even voice. "Kids saw their parents steal, so they thought it was all right. They saw their parents hurt others, so they thought that's what you had to do to prove you were tough. They saw their parents do drugs and get arrested, so it all felt normal to them."

Ethan's eyebrows drew together.

"You don't understand, do you?"

He shook his head.

Cord nodded, as if that proved his point. "That's good. You don't understand because your mother got you out of that place. She got you out of that life." He looked up at Melanie.

Warmth swept her skin. She'd made so many mistakes, yet to hear Cord, she was a heroine. Even though she'd not only cheated Ethan of his dad, she'd cheated Cord of his son.

"But why did she tell me you were dead?"

Her throat ached. That was how she'd felt when Cord had been arrested and throughout the years that followed. As if he was dead. Worse than dead. Because he'd chosen to become something he was not, something that represented the very thing she was trying to purge from her own life.

But that wasn't why she'd told Ethan he was

dead. She'd given Ethan that story so he'd never seek Cord out. So he'd never suffer the disappointment and humiliation she'd felt when she learned Cord had killed someone. When her own father had been hauled away for armed robbery when she was a little girl. "I never should have told you Cord was dead, Ethan."

"When I got arrested, your mom was scared. She didn't want you to grow up like those other kids. She didn't want you to think breaking the law was okay."

"Is lying okay?"

His question ground into her like gravel in an open wound. "Lying isn't okay, either. I was wrong."

Ethan kept his eyes on Cord, acting as if Melanie wasn't even there. "Why didn't *you* tell me? When you found out, why didn't you tell me, too?"

Melanie laid her hand on her son's leg. "Cord only found out a couple of days ago. When he showed up at the house."

Cord held up his hand. "But that doesn't change the fact that I should have told you. We both should have."

Melanie nodded. He was right. There was no way around it.

"Why didn't you?"

"Because it was a lot to handle," Melanie said. "A lot to make sense of all at once."

Ethan's brows pulled together again.

Cord let out a breath. "I didn't think I'd be a good dad, Ethan. That's why *I* didn't tell you."

"Why not?"

"I've done some bad things. I've been in prison. I guess I was as scared about that stuff as your mom."

"Scared that I would be bad, too?"

"I never thought you'd be bad. I just worried that if I was your dad, you'd start thinking all the bad stuff I did was okay."

Ethan stared at his hands.

Seconds ticked by. The boat rolled on the waves. The wind whistled outside. Melanie didn't know what had happened to the others, but the boat was so quiet it felt like she and Cord and Ethan were the only people in the world.

Ethan peered up at Cord. "Do you think it's okay? What *your* dad did?"

Melanie gasped in a breath, feeling as if all the air had been knocked from her lungs. She knew they would have to talk about Kane eventually, but she still wasn't ready. She'd never be ready.

"Your dad is Dryden Kane, right?" Ethan prodded.

Cord nodded calmly. "Yes. I didn't know him growing up, but Dryden Kane is my father."

"Is what he did okay with you?"

"No."

Melanie leaned forward, trying to catch her son's eye. "Of course Cord doesn't think what he did was okay. Nothing about Dryden Kane is okay."

Ethan ignored her, his gaze riveted to Cord. "Are you going to be like him?"

"Never." The word wrenched from Melanie's throat.

"No, Ethan, I'm not," Cord said.

"Am I?"

Melanie rose to her feet. She couldn't believe what he was saying. "No, Ethan. Why would you even think that?"

He finally looked up at her. His eyes narrowed to blue slits. "Because that's what both of you said. That if Cord is my dad, I'm going to do bad things just like him. Then why won't Cord do bad things like Dryden Kane? Why won't I?"

Pain knifed through Melanie's chest, chased by numbness. "That's what I was afraid of, wasn't it?"

Cord nodded. "It's what we were both afraid of."

She sat back down next to Ethan and grasped his hands in hers. Why hadn't this been clear to her before? Why hadn't it occurred to her that she was selling her son short, that in all of this, she never once considered his thoughts and choices and way-too-mature-for-his-years mind?

Cord had been an angry kid. He'd been a kid whose mother was more interested in blocking out her own pain and disappointment than helping her son deal with his. He'd been a kid who'd hadn't believed he was worth much. Ethan wasn't like that. Ethan had never lived that desperate life. He was never wanting for love, never starved for attention. She'd seen to that. Ethan was Ethan. No one else.

How had she forgotten who her own son was?

"I'm so sorry, Ethan. I was wrong to think that. You're your own person. You make your own decisions. Good decisions. You always have."

Ethan met her eyes. He nodded just as his chin started to tremble and fat tears rolled from the corners of his eyes.

She gathered him into her arms. Holding him tightly against her chest, she kissed his forehead and let her tears mix with his. And over Ethan's head, she offered Cord a smile—one she felt deep into the marrow of her bones.

Chapter Thirteen

Cord sat on the edge of the bed and watched his son's chest steadily rise and fall.

His son.

He rolled the weight of those two words around in his mind, feeling them, savoring them. He'd actually felt like a father tonight. Or at least the way he imagined being a father would feel.

And he had Melanie to thank.

She curled next to Ethan, her tears dry, her face peaceful. In Cord's entire life, no one had believed he was worth a damn. No one except Mel. And here she was believing again, after all that had happened, after all he'd done.

He didn't need her encouragement to want to come through for his son. But without it, he never would have dared hope he was able.

As if she sensed his gaze, her eyes fluttered awake. "Hi."

The warm, sleepy whisper of her voice tugged at him. "I thought you were sleeping."

"I was. Dreaming." She stretched and sat up. "Where are you going?"

He didn't want to go anywhere. He wanted to lie down on the bed next to her and let the sway of the boat beneath them lull him into a dream world from which he never had to awake.

Too bad that wasn't possible. "I thought I'd check out the deck."

She climbed out from under the blankets and pulled them over Ethan's shoulders. "I'll come with you."

Cord grabbed a folded blanket from the foot of the bed. Cold had never bothered him, but judging from the sway of the boat and the low hum of wind outside, he doubted jeans and a T-shirt would be enough to keep Mel warm.

He opened the door quietly so as not to wake Ethan, and they slipped out into the kitchen.

They trod lightly through the galley on unsteady legs. Passing the closed door where Bryce and Sylvie slept, they found the steps leading to the deck. Cord pushed the hatch open and they climbed outside.

Their surroundings were quite different from the park where they'd boarded the boat. Where those shores had been rimmed with homes, these were more remote. Not even a sparkle of light broke the dark silhouette of forest rustling in the wind. Probably Governor Nelson State Park on the north rim of the lake. On the aft side of the boat, the far away lights of Madison, the University of Wisconsin campus, and glow of the Capitol dome sparkled on the waves.

They moved to the bow. In front of the glassed-in cab that housed the controls, a bench hooked in a horseshoe. Mel spread out the blanket and sank onto one end of the long bench. Wrapping half the blanket around her shoulders, she held out the other half in an invitation to join her.

Something inside Cord's chest trembled.

"What's wrong?"

"Nothing." Only that he wanted to join her so much he was shaking inside like an awkward teen. Stifling the feeling, he lowered himself to the bench and draped the blanket around his shoulders.

Her scent swirled through him. The gentle glow of moonlight and water shimmered on her skin, making it look soft as brushed silk. Even in the dim light, the faded evidence of freckles danced over the bridge of her nose just as they had when she was a girl.

His fingers twitched. What he wouldn't give to trace those freckles again, to touch that skin.

"He's something, our boy. Isn't he?" she said.

Our boy. His and Melanie's. "He's unbelievable."

She smiled, her whole face glowing with a light he'd never seen. Not even when they were kids themselves. "He was so brave tonight. So strong." She shook her head and pushed out a small derisive laugh. "I wish I had just a sliver of his strength."

"Wish? You do. You're the bravest, strongest woman I've ever known."

She gave him a sideways look. "I sure don't feel it. Ever since this whole thing started, I've been scared to death."

"Listen, it took guts to pull yourself out of the neighborhood we grew up in. Guts to even dare believe you deserved something better. But you did it. For yourself and for our son. You're the reason he's the way he is. You gave him the strength to deal with a father who's an ex-con. And a grandfather..." He couldn't finish.

She covered his hand with hers. "I'm sorry for some of those things I said. About you—"

"Don't you apologize. Those things were true." He shook his head. "I'm the one who's sorry. I'm sorry I let you down."

"You didn't let me down tonight, Cord. Tonight you came through for Ethan." She gave him a watery smile. "And for me."

He sat perfectly still, drinking in her look, her words. All those years in prison, he hadn't believed he could miss her more. He hadn't known how strong the feeling could be until he'd seen her again. And after all they'd shared tonight, the love he felt for Melanie was so much stronger, so much more profound than what they'd had as kids, it pulsed deep inside.

"Do you know what I was dreaming?"

He was almost afraid to ask, but he had to know. "What?"

"I dreamed you were sitting next to me, like now. And you weren't wearing a shirt. And something terrible was going to happen. A bad feeling was hanging in the air, you know? But I didn't have to run or hide or even think. Somehow I knew everything would be okay. That all I had to do was just stay right there tracing the lines of your tattoos with my fingers, and I'd be safe. Everything would work out. Isn't that weird?"

A shiver rippled over his skin. "Pretty weird." He followed Melanie's gaze to the black trees along the shore.

"I missed you, Cord. I didn't know how much until tonight."

"I missed you, too. More than anything else in my life."

She brought her gaze back to his face. Her dark eyes looked into him, past the tattoos, past the rap sheet, until she reached the part no one else had ever seen. "It's lonely being a single parent. Hard."

He nodded, his throat thick. He thought of his mother, the trials he put her through. The mess her life was, even before the extra burden he'd heaped on her shoulders. "I can imagine the problems would be hard to deal with on your own."

"It's not that. I mean, that's true, but the problems aren't the hardest part."

"I can't imagine what's harder."

A wistful smile curved the corners of her lips. "Those moments when Ethan beams a smile at me from left field after making a great catch. Or when he's concentrating on one of his video games so hard that his tongue darts back and forth across his upper lip."

He smiled. "I've seen that."

She snuggled a little deeper into the blanket, a little closer to Cord. "But mostly the times I check on him in the middle of the night, and he's sleeping so perfectly that I'm struck by how much of a miracle he is. And the fact that I made him. And I have no one to share it with. No one in the world who feels the same."

His throat closed. For a moment he didn't talk. He just soaked in her words until they nestled inside him and glowed with quiet understanding. "He *is* a miracle, isn't he?"

Her smile widened, making her whole face shine. "Yeah."

He leaned close to her, soaking in the moment. Despite the cool, fall-tinged wind, his senses swirled with her heat, her scent.

She searched his eyes. Tilting her chin up, she parted her lips. An invitation to be kissed.

An invitation he should refuse.

An invitation he couldn't. He lowered his mouth to hers.

Her lips were as soft and warm as he remembered. Soft and warm as he had dreamed. Yet so real, so tender, they were like nothing he'd ever felt before.

The need for more built inside him like a physical pressure. He slipped his tongue between her lips, coaxing into the depths of her mouth.

She opened to him. Tangling her tongue with his, she encouraged him deeper. As if she too needed to be closer. As if she'd missed him as much as he'd missed her.

He explored her mouth and nipped her lips. He couldn't get enough of her, the taste, the feel. He drew in breath after breath of her. He wanted to take her, absorb her so he'd never again lose her. So neither one of them would ever again be alone.

Her fingers moved under his shirt, warm on his skin.

The pressure built. The need to touch. To taste.

To claim. He slipped his hands under her T-shirt and skimmed up her sides, over soft skin, over the even ridges of her ribs. Catching the stiff underwire cupping her breasts, he pushed her bra up and over. One soft mound fell free, then the other. He took them in his hands. Her nipples jutted taut between his fingers.

She arched her back, pushing her breasts into his hands. She trailed her fingers over his skin. As if she couldn't get enough, either. As if she had missed his heat, his scent, as much as he'd missed her.

He released her long enough to peel her shirt over her head. He unhooked her bra and slipped the straps down her arms.

The blanket fell off their shoulders. Cool air swirled around them. Moonlight caressed Melanie's hair, her face, the full curves of her breasts.

An ache filled his groin, so hot and hard he nearly groaned. It had been so long since he'd been with a woman, but this wasn't just any woman. Melanie was the only woman he wanted. The only woman he'd fantasized about all those years of lying on the steel tray in his cell. The only woman whose voice cried out in his dreams.

Skimming up her sides with his hands, he cupped both breasts. His splayed fingers looked rough and dark against her skin. He rolled and pinched her nipples between thumb and forefinger until he could feel the moan building in her chest.

"Cord." Pleasure deepened her voice, giving the sound a guttural, primal urgency.

Heat broke over him in waves. He wanted to be closer. He wanted to taste her. He wanted to be inside.

He lifted her breasts, mounding them, pointing her dusky nipples up to meet his mouth. He ran his tongue over one taut nub and then the other.

He'd dreamed of her sweet scent. Dreamed of the sound of her voice, the feel of her skin. But no dream was this vivid, this real. No memory of her teenage body came close to the woman's body he held in his arms right now.

She moved her hands lower, unsnapping, unzipping, pushing into his jeans. The warmth of her fingers closed around him.

Blood surged to his groin. Desire burned through him, almost as much pain as pleasure. He'd waited so long. He wanted this so much.

She shoved down his waistband and lifted him out into the cool air.

The wind swept over him, fanning the flame, making him burn even hotter. He wanted to bury himself in her wet heat. He wanted to lose himself and never be found again.

"I want you, Cord. I always have. As hard as I tried, I never stopped wanting you."

And he wanted her. Wanted her like nothing before. Needed her more than food or water or air.

Maybe it was possible. Maybe anything was possible. At least tonight.

He moved his hand down to her jeans. Unbuttoning and unzipping with clumsy fingers, he pushed the denim over the soft curve of her hips and down her legs. Her panties were a slip of silky, lacy stuff, something he might find sexy in a less heated moment. Now he just wanted them off, wanted them gone. Now they seemed like nothing but an affront to the perfection of her bare skin.

He slipped his hand under the lace and skimmed the panty down her legs. Depositing the lace on the deck along with her jeans, he smoothed his hands back up her legs until he reached the heat between her thighs.

She was wet and hot and everything he needed. He pushed his fingers between her folds, moving back and forth against her, feeling the way she opened and met his thrusts.

Another moan shook her.

He closed his lips over hers, trapping the sound, keeping it for his own.

She shuddered, moving faster. Her hand closed tighter around him, moving up and down his shaft in crazy rhythm.

He gritted his teeth. He couldn't lose it. Not

yet. He wanted to be inside her again. Part of her. He wanted to taste every sensation and lock it away to keep forever.

He grabbed her hand, stilling her movement. Burying his fingers in her hair, he drew her to him, kissing her deeply.

She gripped his shoulders and kneeled on the bench. Throwing one leg over his lap, she straddled him, opening herself over him. Her breasts surged into his face.

He skimmed his hands up her body and gathered her breasts together in his hands. Burying his mouth between them, he breathed deeply, brushing his lips against her soft skin.

Her hand found his length. She lowered herself and rubbed his tip against her wetness, her warmth. Positioning him at her gateway, she lowered further, taking him inside.

A groan vibrated in his chest. He tilted his hips upward, reaching for her, pushing himself fully home.

Just where he had to be.

Just where—at this moment—he could almost believe he belonged.

CORD WOKE TO THE THRUM of the boat's engine. He glanced at the glowing hands of his watch. He and Mel had only returned to the cabin an hour ago to sleep next to their son. It didn't make sense that the boat was already moving. They were supposed to remain anchored until this afternoon, when they would take Melanie and Ethan to the airport and he would go to the florist and bakery.

The sudden change of plans couldn't be good.

He crept from the bed, careful not to wake Mel or their son. Pausing a moment, he let his gaze linger on the perfection of her face. Last night was more than he'd ever believed possible. He'd been in love with Mel forever, and still he'd never known what love could be until last night. And if it was possible for everything to work out, for the police to catch Kane, for life to return to normal, he had the feeling his life might even turn around. That it would only get better from here.

He soaked in the way her hair fanned over the pillow, dark on light. The slope of her cheekbones. The smile playing at her lips. He could stare at her for hours. Days. A lifetime.

For the first time in his life, he could actually hope.

The pitch of the boat's engine dropped, slowing as if approaching a dock. Scooping in one more glance at Mel's face and breath of her scent, he slipped out of the cabin and found his way to the deck.

Bryce Walker sat alone behind the wheel. He

piloted the vessel along a row of houses and through the no-wake zone leading to a park—a different park than where they had boarded the boat last night. McCaskey and Diana stood at the end of the pier that ran alongside the boat landing.

Cord stepped up behind Walker. "What's going on?" he yelled over the engine.

Walker whipped around. Seeing Cord, he let out a relieved breath and turned his focus back to the approaching pier. "Change of plans."

So Walker was as tense as he was. "I see that. Why?"

"Reed's call. That's all I know."

They closed the distance to the pier. Grabbing one of the tie lines, McCaskey pulled the boat close, and he and Diana climbed aboard.

"Take us out," McCaskey said to Walker. "I don't want to take any chances."

The bad feeling that had assaulted Cord at the first sound of the engine grew stronger. Something had happened. Something big.

After heading out to deeper water and rounding a peninsula, McCaskey held up a hand. Walker set the anchor and switched off the engine, and the four of them took seats on the horseshoe bench where Melanie and Cord had made love just a short time ago.

Cord focused on McCaskey, trying not to think

of what he and Mel had shared. As wonderful as their night together had been, as warm as the hope was blossoming in his imagination, they wouldn't be able to share anything unless the problem of Dryden Kane could be solved. He had to stay focused or he wouldn't have to worry about the future. He wouldn't have one.

None of them would. "What happened?"

McCaskey leaned forward, elbows on knees. "We found another body."

Walker sat back in the bench and raked a hand through his brown hair. "Kane's handiwork?" He looked tired, as if Kane's relentless evil was getting to him, wearing him out.

McCaskey gave a nod.

Cord balled his hands into fists. It was hard enough to protect Melanie, Ethan and his sisters. It was impossible to protect every woman in the area. Kane would always be one step ahead of police. That's why Nikki Valducci's idea of setting a trap for him had made so much sense. "So are you ready to help Kane with his reception?"

McCaskey's head dipped. When he returned his gaze to Cord's, his jaw was hard with determination. "Yes. But we have a slight change."

"Change? Why?"

"The body we found. It was Janet Blankenship's."

Foreboding slid through Cord's veins.

Walker looked from one to the other. "Are you planning to fill me in? Who's Janet Blankenship?"

"Her car followed us last night."

"Her car." Walker nodded, mental wheels turning. "So it was Kane behind the wheel."

McCaskey gave a nod.

"He didn't see the boat, did he?" Walker asked.

"He kept going on the highway when we turned off," McCaskey explained. "He must have realized we'd spotted him. But he might have recognized the car in the parking lot. From there he could have figured out we were out on the water. Whatever he knows or suspects, he came too close."

Cord shook his head. "An understatement. It's like the bastard is invisible or something. Like he can go anywhere he damn well pleases."

"You ready to move up the timetable, Turner?"

"Hell, yeah." But he had the creeping feeling that moving up the timetable wasn't going to be enough. "What do you have in mind?"

"You get off the boat with me back at the park. Nikki will drop off a rental car at a different location for Melanie and Ethan later this afternoon."

"Why the change?"

"If Kane does suspect we're using a boat, I don't want him to be able to figure out where that boat will dock. And I want to keep him busy during the time Melanie and Ethan fly out. I moved their flight to this evening."

"When I'll be meeting Kane. I'm the decoy."

"Exactly."

So the time to leave was already here. Cold burrowed into his chest. He sucked in a breath, trying to push the sensation away. He couldn't think of what could have been or even what might be in the future. He had to concentrate. He had to pull off this wedding reception plan. The future of everyone on this boat hinged on that.

"Meredith Unger told you the flowers and cake would be ready by four, right?"

"Right. And from there, I'll receive instructions about where to take them."

Reed nodded. "Okay. As soon as you know the location, you tell me. Kane might be watching you, so don't use your cell phone. Just talk into this." He pulled a small microphone from his briefcase.

"I wear that?"

"It clips to your shirt. You won't be able to hear us, but we can hear you."

Cord took the tiny device between thumb and forefinger. "What about an earpiece to go with it? Don't you have something tiny that would fit into my ear? They have them on television."

"Detectives on TV can solve complicated crimes in an hour, too."

"Work on that, will ya?"

"Sure thing."

Cord let out a chuckle. If someone had told him just a few days ago that he would be spending a Sunday morning sitting on a small yacht joking around with a cop, he wouldn't have believed it. But the levity felt good. As if he wasn't about to embark on a potential suicide mission.

Cord forced his mind back to Kane's reception. "So once I tell you the location, what are you going to do?"

"Madison's SWAT and the county's TRT will search the surrounding buildings, and we hope to find out where Kane is before you arrive."

"That's not going to work. Kane has to have thought of that. He's going to be gone as soon as he sees the first blue vest."

Diana sat forward on the bench and nodded. "He's right, Reed. You just don't want to hear it."

"I don't want a repeat of last time."

"It worked."

"We were lucky. I don't want whether you live or die to be decided by luck this time."

Cord shook his head. Obviously McCaskey and Diana's discussion was still going on this morning—a discussion that must have started with her experience with Kane in Banesbridge Prison. "We decided this last night. I go. Alone."

Diana shook her blond head. "Meredith Unger said you were supposed to bring us with you."

"I don't care what she said. I'm not bringing either of you. I'll face Kane alone."

Walker held up his hands. "Whoa. You're not going to walk in without police, are you?"

"Damn straight, I am. As soon as Kane sees cops, he's gone." He held up a hand to silence his sister before she started. "And there's no reason to risk your life, Diana. Kane chose me because he thought he could use me to get to you. I think it's a bad idea to do anything Kane wants. Don't you?"

She frowned and leaned back.

"You're a good man, Turner." McCaskey gave him a nod that conveyed respect and admiration and gratitude all at once. The type of nod Cord had never gotten from anyone but Mel, certainly not from a cop. "You pick up the flowers and cake, then head to wherever the hell Kane sends you. As soon as we hear from you, we'll be ready to roll."

Since McCaskey's little speech that night in the hotel, Cord had tried not to think too much about killing Kane. He couldn't avoid it any longer. Every time he turned around, Kane was right next to him. Every time he took a breath, Kane was within striking distance of Mel and Ethan, Diana and Sylvie. Today it was all going to end. Whatever it took. "As soon as I learn his location, I'll let you know where to pick him up." And if he had to pump a couple of bullets into the serial killer's skull to restrain him until police arrived, so be it.

Chapter Fourteen

Melanie let the hot water cascade over her in the boat's cramped shower, rinsing off shampoo and soap as quickly as she could. The boat's motor thrummed through the cabin like a steady heartbeat. She couldn't believe she'd slept so long. She'd been tired, exhausted really, but that didn't make sleeping until midmorning a good idea. When she awoke, the bed next to her was empty. Cord was already up.

She jumped out of the shower and wrapped a towel around herself. Just the thought of Cord brought a smile to her lips. Her body was deliciously sore from their time on the deck together. And for a moment she just stood in the steam, reliving the feelings. The rasp of Cord's stubbled chin on her tender breasts. The thrust of him inside her, stretching her, completing her.

She wanted to see him. The need to talk to him

this morning pressed down upon her like a gnawing hunger. Soon she and Ethan would be flying out. Until then she wanted to be with Cord every second she could.

She walked back into the cabin where Ethan still slept. After she was dressed, she'd wake him. She hated to do it. They'd gotten so little sleep lately, they would have to sleep away the first two days of Disney World to catch up.

She stepped to the corner where Cord had piled their duffel bags. Reaching for hers, she realized something was missing. Her bag was there. And Ethan's.

But Cord's was gone.

He was supposed to take them to the airport before he lured Kane to the police trap. So why was his bag missing?

She pulled on a light sweater and clean pair of jeans. Shoving her feet into shoes, she struggled to remain calm.

He wouldn't leave. Not without saying goodbye.

She closed the door of the cabin and raced up the stairs to the deck. A cool breeze hit her face. The scent of autumn lurked in the air even though the trees were still summer-green. She scanned the deck, her gaze landing on the group assembled in the bow of the boat. Gripping the rail, she made her way toward them.

The boat closed in on the shore. A different park from last night. Bryce shut off the boat's engine, letting the forward momentum carry them to the dock.

Melanie reached Cord just as he prepared to get off the boat. "You're leaving?"

He turned around fast, as if he'd been caught doing something he knew was wrong.

"You were going to leave without saying goodbye?" She couldn't believe it. She looked at Reed standing with Cord. Bryce and Cord's sisters stood to the side, obviously not planning to disembark. "What's going on?"

Cord focused on her with serious eyes. "That car following us last night. It was Kane."

She sucked in a breath. "Does he know where we are?"

"There's a chance," Reed said. "So I booked you a later flight."

Cord nodded. "A flight that leaves while Kane is meeting me."

The details shifted and fell into place. "So this is goodbye." The last word caught in her throat, almost too painful to say.

Cord glanced at Reed. "I need a few minutes."

Reed nodded.

Taking her hand, Cord led her to the back of the boat where they were alone.

She leaned against the back rail, propping herself against the cold steel for support. She knew that after last night, saying goodbye to Reed today was going to be tough. But at least she'd thought she would have a little time to work up to the moment. "What about Ethan? What should I tell him?"

"I suppose you should tell him the truth."

He was right. She couldn't lie to her son. Not after all they'd been through. But she would have to choose her words carefully. He was still only ten years old. Too young to deal with the fear of knowing what his newly discovered father was about to face.

She wasn't sure she could deal with it. "Do you really have to do this? I mean, isn't there another way?"

"I have to end this, Mel. I'm not going to take the chance that Kane will reach you. Any of you. I have to stop him now."

She studied his squared shoulders, the hard set of his mouth, the regret in his eyes. A tremble filled her, making her feel sick, making her feel weak. "You don't have to take him on yourself, though, right? Reed will be there. The SWAT team."

He hesitated, then nodded.

Why the hesitation? What was he not saying? "The police *are* going to be with you the whole time, aren't they Cord?"

"They'll be there."

"But not the whole time?"

"Kane is not going to hurt me. That I can promise you."

"Because you're going to hurt him first?"

"If I have to."

If he had to. That was self-defense, right? The only problem was that she knew Cord. She knew how he'd handled things before. On his own. Not trusting others. He'd been working with Reed the last few days, working with the police, but that didn't mean he'd changed. It didn't mean he wouldn't take things into his own hands again. "I don't want to lose you again. Not to Kane and not to prison."

"I know. I don't want to lose you, either. Or Ethan. That's why I have to do whatever it takes."

Even if Kane isn't an imminent threat? Even if the law sees it as murder?

She couldn't panic. She couldn't jump to conclusions. She couldn't expect the worst of Cord before even giving him a chance. Wasn't that what his mother had always done? Wasn't that what Mel herself had done with Ethan? She'd expected the worst without really giving him a chance. Without trusting him.

If she really loved Cord, she would have to trust him.

She reached a shaking hand to Cord's shoulder.

She stroked his neck with her fingertips. "Remember us, okay? You have a bright future. *We* have a bright future together. Come back to us."

His eyes glistened. Swallowing hard, he nodded. "I love you, Mel."

"I love you too, Cord. And I trust you to do the right thing. I believe in you. Please believe in yourself, too."

He leaned down and fit his lips to hers. And when the kiss was done, he turned and walked to the front of the boat without looking back.

"Goodbye, Cord," she whispered. Then she headed back to the cabin.

Back to her son.

NIKKI VALDUCCI KNEW ENOUGH not to ask why Reed wanted her to drop off a rental car at the University of Wisconsin's Memorial Union. She didn't want to know. Not with the investigation into the media leak at the police department.

She felt horrible about the suspicion coming down on Stan Perreth's head. God knew the detective was a prick with a capitol *P,* but he wasn't responsible for the leak. She knew it.

Because she was.

She switched off the car's ignition and leaned her head against the steering wheel. Of course, the whole thing had backfired horribly. She'd done it to catch Kane, not help him. She'd used the media to draw him to the police so they could nail the son of a bitch. But no one would believe that now.

She'd been trying to be the hero. She'd been trying to skirt around Reed's stubborn refusal to do anything proactive to nail Kane.

And she'd screwed the pooch.

Her head ached and her stomach writhed, but there was nothing she could do about it now. Nothing but do everything she could to make sure Reed's plan was successful.

That and pray the leak investigation dried up as thoroughly as the Brewers' World Series hopes.

She opened the door. If Reed asked her to drop off a car and hike back to State Street to meet her ride, it was the least she could do. She stepped a foot onto the pavement and started to climb out.

A hand grabbed her wrist.

She reached for her gun. Cold pierced through her right shoulder. *A knife.* Cutting. Slashing. Pain jetted down her arm. She tried to grip the gun. Tried to pull it from her holster, but her fingers wouldn't grip.

He must have severed ligaments. Nerves. Damn, damn, damn. How had she let herself get so distracted? How had she been so deep in her own thoughts that she hadn't seen him?

It didn't matter. Screw him. She wasn't going down without a fight.

She brought her left elbow back and hard into his gut.

Air exploded from his mouth. His grip on her left wrist tightened, he jammed her hand back.

The bones crunched as they snapped. Pain seared up her left arm and spun in her mind. Hot. Cold.

She threw her body toward him, slamming her forehead against his. The force stung her mind and vibrated down her neck.

He stumbled back. For a second he released her shattered wrist.

She brought her knee up.

He blocked her with his thigh, but the blow still brought a grunt.

She didn't hesitate. She launched into him again, battering with her useless hands, driving her boot into his shin.

He shoved her, back against the car. Clutching at her waist, he pulled out her gun. He thrust the barrel against her head.

She froze and looked at him for the first time. It could have been a mugger. A rapist. But somehow she knew it wasn't. Without looking, without thinking, she'd known her attacker was Dryden Kane.

His cold blue eyes stared at her, inches away. His minty breath fanned her cheek. He had dyed his hair again, this time blond, and shaved his beard, but she couldn't help recognizing the face she'd been obsessed with for more than a year.

The face she'd planned to build her career on. "I'm a cop, you bastard."

"Should I be afraid?"

She scanned the parking lot with her periphery vision, trying to spot someone, anyone who could help. A group of girls headed along the lake on their way to the Union Terrace. A few others made their way down Langdon toward State Street. No one seemed to notice the serial killer, the gun at her head. It was as if they were invisible.

Or maybe the kids were too scared to risk getting involved.

She looked straight at him. If he wanted to see fear from her, he was out of luck. If he wanted her to beg for her life and scream loud enough to turn him on, he'd come to the wrong woman. She glanced at the bruise blooming on his forehead and smiled. "You're going down, Kane."

"I see what you mean. My situation looks pretty dire, doesn't it?" He gave her a shove, pushing her into the car and facedown on the console between the bucket seats. He shoved his knee into her back and leaned on her with all his weight.

Pain shot up her spine. She sucked in a breath and tensed her abdominal muscles, trying to compensate for the downward pressure.

"The people in this town are so damn dumb. They don't think anything can hurt them. They're looking at us now and thinking that we're playing some sort of sex game. And you know what? They're right." He rummaged at her waist and pulled out her handcuffs. Wrenching each arm behind her back, he tightened them down.

Pain rocketed through her broken wrist and up her arm. She breathed hard through her mouth, in and out like a woman in heavy labor.

"It's not just the people who are so damn dumb. You cops think you can fool me? You think you can dangle a little meat in front of me and I'll bite like some kind of animal?"

The trap Reed and Cord Turner had set. He must be talking about the trap.

"You cops are so predictable. Always trying to get something for nothing. I name a location, and you all jump. But McCaskey can't bring himself to take a risk. He can't bring himself to bait his trap with something I really want."

He let up on the knee. Grabbing a handful of hair, he pulled, lifting Nikki up and forcing her into the passenger seat. He climbed behind the wheel. "I knew he wouldn't risk letting Cordell bring Diana to me. I knew he would try to outsmart me. Idiot. Hasn't he figured out anything?"

Her scalp stung. Her wrist throbbed, pinched

behind her against the seat. Pain rushed hot and real into her shoulder.

"All I had to do was watch. All I had to do was wait for someone to make a move. McCaskey. You."

So he'd targeted her. He'd been following her from the very beginning.

"All I had to do was keep my eye on the ball. Or should I say, the boat?" He looked out at the lake, calm and black in the dusk. "Who are you meeting here, Detective Valducci?"

She clamped her mouth shut. She wouldn't tell him even if she knew.

"I know it's not Cordell. He's setting his pitiful trap. Could it be my grandson? Could it be Sylvie or her husband the counselor?" He smacked his lips. "Or is it Diana? Daddy's little girl."

Nikki thought she might throw up. "You are one sick bastard."

He gave her hair a yank.

A groan escaped from her lips despite her efforts to choke it back.

"Does that hurt?" The glow of excitement lit his face, though his eyes were dead and cold as ever.

He was trying to scare her. Hurt her. Fear and pain and domination. That's what he got off on. She set her chin. He wasn't going to get off on her. "It just takes my mind off the other pain. I hope you're not waiting for a scream. I hate to disappoint."

He leaned close to her ear, as if ready to whisper an intimate secret. "Try this." He took her lobe between his teeth and bit down.

She could hear the layers of skin pop. Heat trickled sticky down her neck.

He pulled back and watched her face as if soaking in her expression. Her blood glistened on his lips. "Who are you meeting? Diana? Sylvie? The boy and his hot little mother?"

Pain screamed through her nerves, so loud it made her numb. He could do whatever he wanted, but she wasn't going to tell him a thing. She'd already helped him when she hadn't intended to. She wasn't going to help him knowingly, not even to save her own skin. "Go to hell, you miserable, inadequate worm."

A vein throbbed on the side of his neck, but his expression still didn't change.

It didn't matter. She knew she'd hit bone. She'd lived and breathed this bastard for too long not to know how to hurt him. And if she hurt him badly enough, maybe he would forget to wonder why she was here. Maybe he would drive her to some remote location to prove his manliness *before* Diana or Sylvie or Melanie and the kid arrived for the car.

Maybe she could do something to make up for the mistakes she made.

Gun still on her, he retrieved the knife from the

backseat floor. He held it up in the parking lot lights, the blood from her shoulder still wet on the blade. "Should I kill you right now? Let you bleed out all over the interior of your rental car?"

She forced calm into her screaming mind. "That seems kind of easy."

"Easy, huh? When I cut you, your heart will keep beating. Your mind will keep working. You'll feel every bit of pain. You'll be able to look down and see me as I work."

She choked back her revulsion and focused on what she had to do. "The stress really is getting to you, isn't it? You're decompensating. You're losing it. I thought you liked the hunt, Kane. I thought you liked to prove you were dominant. Or are you afraid to hunt a cop? A *woman* cop? Are you afraid I'll kick your ass and prove what a sorry, inadequate piece of shit you really are?"

His fist lashed out, hitting her square in the face.

Her head snapped back. The sting ripped through her skull and rang in her ears. Everything around her flickered, and the world went black.

Chapter Fifteen

Cord stepped out of his car, carrying cake in one hand and a box of rose and baby's breath corsages in the other. The parking lot of Olbrich Gardens was empty. The building housing the indoor garden and other facilities was dark. Balancing both boxes in one arm, he tried the glass doors. Locked.

He didn't have to open the lid of the sheet cake and compare to know that he'd come to the right place. The picture on the top of the cake, a garden wedding recreated in icing and sprayed color was a direct replica of the Olbrich gates and gardens beyond.

Maybe that was it. Maybe he needed to enter through the gate.

It was a nice trick, loading him down with cake and flowers, keeping his hands full. But what Kane couldn't see was the gun he held beneath the sheet cake. The knife he'd stashed among the corsages.

From his brief discussion with his sisters last night, he'd gathered that Sylvie and Bryce Walker had been married here in the gardens. No doubt that was part of the reason Kane had picked this location. Diana and Reed had been married on the beach. Too public. But as long as the gardens were closed, they could be a lonely, isolated place. A place where Kane could have his way.

Cord pushed the gate with his shoulder. It swung open easily. Every nerve on alert, he slipped inside and scanned the manicured lawn and early fall flowers for signs of movement, signs of anything.

Growing up in the city, he'd never spent much time in gardens. But one look at this place, and he knew Melanie would love it. The meandering paths. The pointed roof of a gazebo peeking out from a rose garden. The perfect setting for a wedding.

But he couldn't think about Melanie now. About the last words she'd said. About the plane that would be taking off soon, whisking her and Ethan to Florida.

He loved her with all his heart. For him, there had never been anyone else. But as much as he'd like to believe in that bright future together that she'd talked about, he couldn't manage it. Not yet. Not until the shadow of Dryden Kane was no longer blocking the sun.

MELANIE PUT HER ARM around Ethan as the boat cruised toward shore. Up ahead, the lights of the Memorial Union Terrace glowed through the dusk. Next door the fat turrets of the Red Gym jutted dark into the air, an old castle in the middle of the University of Wisconsin campus.

Reed had called to say a rental sedan would be waiting in the parking lot between the Red Gym and the Union, the keys under the seat. After they picked up the car, just a short drive to the airport and they'd be boarding a plane to Disney World and far away from Dryden Kane.

And Cord.

Melanie had tried not to think about him, tried not to wonder where he was, what danger he was facing, but it was no use. Even prayer hadn't helped the way it had in the past. Nothing had helped but thinking of Ethan. His safety. His happiness. As long as Ethan was all right, she could survive anything. She had to survive anything. Even losing Cord.

She smiled at the excitement in her son's face as they neared the shore and their trip to Disney. She hadn't told him about Cord yet. She hadn't said a word. And she kept hoping that maybe she wouldn't have to. Maybe the police would catch Kane and everything would turn out okay.

The easy, laid-back rhythm of a reggae band

echoed across the water from the Terrace, growing louder the closer they got to shore. It was unusual for the Terrace to be hosting a Sunday evening band, but she had to admit it was nice. As if a festive send off would make for a happy trip.

"Have a good time at Disney." Diana smiled at Ethan.

Sylvie's eyebrow ring twinkled in the light from the city. "I hope we can see you when you get back."

Melanie pushed back another surge of tears. They hadn't had much of a chance to get to know Cord's sisters, but what she'd learned about them made her want to know more. They and their husbands seemed like good people. People who had been through hell and had survived. People who'd once been lonely but had forged family ties stronger than just the blood the sisters shared.

"I'd like that." She offered the twins a smile, then glanced at Ethan. "We sure wouldn't want to miss seeing the baby when it's born."

Ethan nodded. "Where's Cord? I mean, Dad?"

Melanie knelt down in front of him. "Your dad had to help Reed."

He eyed her as if he'd picked up wind of her unease.

"We'll talk more on the plane, okay, honey?"

Ethan nodded. "Okay."

Bryce cut the engine. The boat drifted toward a

pier flanked with sailboats and rental canoes. Its forward momentum had almost stopped when it bumped against the rubber on the pier's edge.

Emerging from behind the controls. Bryce gave Melanie and Ethan a smile. "I can't tell you how glad we are that our little guy is going to have a cousin like you."

"Girl. Our little girl," Sylvie teased.

Bryce chuckled. "Right. Now, have a great time at Disney. Check out the haunted house for me, will you?"

Ethan grinned. "You bet."

Bryce made his way to the ladder and climbed down to the pier to secure the boat.

Melanie traded hugs with Diana and Sylvie. Putting her arm back around her son's shoulders, she ushered him to the ladder and peered over the edge.

Bryce lay facedown on the pier. Red covered the back of his shirt, was smeared over the white boards.

Was he hurt? Had he fallen?

Or was he—

A hand jutted up from the ladder and grabbed her wrist.

She looked down into the barrel of a gun—and the eyes of Dryden Kane.

Chapter Sixteen

Cord walked along the cobblestone garden paths for what had to be the fortieth time. He'd covered much of the sixteen acres of outdoor gardens, the Thai Pavilion, the rose garden, the formal English garden. And while his appreciation for plants and gardening had taken a great leap forward, his patience had disappeared. Kane wasn't here. And Cord had the feeling the serial killer wasn't planning to be.

Approaching the gate and turnstile, he dipped his chin to the microphone clamped to the inside of his shirt collar. "I'm at Olbrich Gardens. Either Kane is playing some game I'm missing, or he's a no-show."

He made his way back to the gate, arriving just as a green sedan pulled into the parking lot. He reached the car before Reed McCaskey climbed out. "So much for our trap."

McCaskey's eyebrows dipped and worry lines

dug into his forehead. "Diana was right. If she was here, Kane wouldn't have the choice. He'd have to come."

"You still have the SWAT team on standby?"

He nodded. "They're searching the surrounding buildings and perimeter. There's one thing that worries me."

He raised his brows and waited for McCaskey to continue.

"If Kane isn't here, where is he?"

"That's a damn good question." He looked at his watch. He had something to do first. Something that couldn't wait. "I'm going to the airport. I want to make sure Mel and Ethan are on that plane."

McCaskey nodded. "Nikki dropped a blue late model Taurus at the Memorial Union over an hour ago. They should have picked it up and arrived at the airport by now. If something happened, Bryce would have called me."

"Maybe so, but I'm not going to assume anything. I have to know for sure."

"The plane takes off in fifteen minutes. You won't make it in time. I'll call."

"Go ahead. But I'll probably get my answer before you get off hold."

"FLIGHT 1165? I'm sorry, it already departed."

Cord looked at the older woman behind the

airport baggage-check-in counter. After waiting in line for what seemed like an eternity, he was ready to crawl out of his skin and down her throat. Not her fault. This had to be the most popular night to fly out of Madison in history. Why? He had no clue. He probably should have waited for Mc-Caskey to call, although he might be having the same luck. "I know the plane took off. I just need to know if two passengers were on it."

She looked up over the line of people waiting to check their suitcases. "Well, I'm afraid we're really busy. If you come back in—"

"I'm not waiting." His voice boomed out, harsher than he intended.

Penciled eyebrows arched in surprise.

He held his hands in front of him, palms out. "I'm sorry. I didn't mean to yell. But this is very urgent. I have to know if Melanie and Ethan Frist were aboard that flight. And I have to know now."

Blowing a sigh through her pointed nose, she slipped on a pair of reading glasses that were dangling on a chain around her neck. "Melanie what?"

"Frist. And her son Ethan."

She squinted at the computer monitor. Pushing keys as if in slow motion, she hummed under her breath.

"Were they on the flight?"

"Well…"

"Well, what? Please."

She peered at him over her glasses. "It seems they never checked in."

"A FORMER FRIEND of mine recently pointed out how I've been in such a hurry, I haven't stopped to smell the roses. You know, I haven't really taken the time to enjoy the things I love to do. I think it's good advice. We should all stop and smell the roses from time to time, don't you think?"

Melanie choked back the thick, tinny taste of fear clogging her throat and forced herself to stay calm. She, Ethan, Diana and Sylvie lay propped on the bed where Sylvie and Bryce had slept last night. Ropes bit into her wrists and bruised her ankles. But she'd guess the pain of her ligatures was nothing compared with the handcuffs Kane had used to secure Diana.

Judging from the red-purple color of her fingers, Kane had tightened them to the point of cutting off her circulation, steel cutting into flesh. And the bruise along her cheek and eye where Kane had clubbed her to gain her cooperation was turning a similar color.

On the other side of Diana, Kane finished securing Sylvie's hands and moved to her legs. She'd already been sick, the poor woman. And now she looked as pale as death.

Melanie shifted closer to Ethan who huddled between her and Diana. He hadn't said a word, hadn't made a sound, but she could feel him shaking. The evidence of his fear and her inability to soothe it away ate into her like acid.

Kane tightened the rope around Sylvie's ankles and continued his taunting drone. "It was so nice of your husband to lend me his boat, don't you think? Out here on the water, I have time. Time to relax. Time to enjoy my family."

"Family. Family is about more than blood. You're not family. You're a monster." Sylvie jerked her feet to the side, pulling them from Kane's grasp.

He lashed out with a hand, slapping her.

Sylvie's head jerked to the side. The sound cracked in the cabin as loud as a gunshot. Blood bloomed red in the corner of her mouth. She stared straight ahead, stunned. Tears streaked over her reddening cheek.

"It seems it would serve you well to know your place, Sylvia. To obey your father."

"You're no father of mine."

He hit her again.

Sylvie reeled to the side, the force sending her off the edge of the bed. She hit the floor with a thump.

"Believe me, that hurt me far more than it hurt you. You can stay down there until you learn some manners. Or until I'm tired of having you around."

"Let them go, Kane. It's me you want." Diana's voice boomed strong, as if she hadn't noticed she was bruised and battered and tied hand and foot.

"Didn't I tell you to call me Daddy?" His lips pulled back from his perfect teeth in a smile. "You are my favorite, of course. But what about your sister? If I give you all the attention, she's bound to get jealous. And sibling jealousy can be so nasty."

"Then just take us," Sylvie's muffled voice rose from the floor.

Melanie let out a breath. At least she was okay. For now.

"Take you? And not my grandson?" He rounded the bed, eyeing Ethan with the wide-eyed focus of a psychopath.

Despite Melanie's best effort to keep quiet, a sound vibrated in her throat, low and guttural.

Kane stepped to Melanie's side of the bed. He pulled his knife from the sheath on his belt. Dried blood dulled the blade.

She choked back a scream, pressing it down, compressing the fear until it hardened into anger inside her. He wasn't going to touch Ethan. She didn't know how she'd stop him, but she'd find a way. "Touch my son and you're dead."

Kane's lips thinned. One corner quirked into a smile. "I'm not going to hurt my grandson. What kind of a monster do you think I am?"

She'd warned Cord not to kill Kane, not unless he had to, not unless he was under imminent attack. But if she had a gun right this minute, she knew in her heart she could shoot. More than that. If he escaped she would chase after him, hunt him down and kill him in cold blood.

Kane leaned his face toward hers. The cool scent of mint carried by his breath fanned her face. "I'm not going to kill my grandson. I'm going to train him. I'm going to show him what life is all about. Life *and* death. I've always wanted to be immortal, to go on even after I die. And the way I see it, with the proper training, Ethan is my legacy."

Chapter Seventeen

Cord scanned car after car in the parking lot between the Memorial Union and the Red Gym. SUVs, vans and sports cars. But not one of them was a Taurus. Not one.

He wiped his palms on his jeans and tried to breathe. When he'd heard Melanie and Ethan hadn't checked in for their flight, he'd been hoping they'd stayed on the boat. That they'd gotten stalled in the middle of the lake, missed the time, something. Anything.

But if they were still on the boat, the car would be here. Wouldn't it? If they'd changed plans for any reason, Bryce Walker would have called McCaskey. He would have let them know. Wouldn't he?

Of course, maybe he had.

Cord grabbed the cell phone from his belt and punched in McCaskey's number.

The detective answered on the first ring. "Yeah?"

"Have you talked to Walker?"

"Can't reach him. I've also been trying to find Nikki and get through to the airport. Melanie and Ethan? Are they off?"

"They never made it to the plane."

"Oh, hell. Where are you now?"

"At the Union. There's no Taurus here."

"Maybe they were delayed. An accident. A flat tire."

He'd like to believe the explanation was something so reasonable. He'd like to, but he couldn't. "Are you sure Nikki dropped off the car?"

"That's what I've been trying to find out, but she's not answering radio or phone."

"What if something happened to her? What if she never dropped it off?"

"Bryce should have called."

How could a car disappear? How could it be that they couldn't get ahold of anyone who knew what was going on?

He eyed the stretch of lakefront behind the Memorial Union. College kids sat at tables and balanced on the edge of concrete planters, watching a reggae band perform on the Union Terrace's outdoor stage. There had to be something he could do. Some way to get answers. He just had to come up with what. "Listen there is a band playing. Lots of kids. Someone would have had to see a boat that big. Someone would have noticed. I'm going to ask around." Cord lowered the phone.

"Wait."

He clapped it back against his ear. "What?"

"The rental. I'll bet it has GPS. Let me check. Hold on."

Cord forced himself to slow down. To breathe. Still holding the phone to his ear, he started for the Union Terrace. A mix of students and alumni and just plain citizens crowded around tables and sat on the trademark sunburst chairs. A girl shot past him, carrying a pitcher of beer to a table of friends.

Cord started after her. "Excuse me."

"Turner? You still there?"

Cord gave up his pursuit. He held his hand against his other ear, straining to hear over the reggae beat. "Did you locate the car?"

"It's at Picnic Point. It's not moving."

Dread stabbed into him, cold and hopeless. There was only one reason for the car to be parked in an out-of-the-way location like that.

Were they still alive?

If that bastard had touched Ethan or Melanie—

He pinched the bridge of his nose between thumb and forefinger. "What's the fastest way to Picnic Point from here?"

"Several units in the area are already on their

way. It's not far, but they'll still get there long before you will."

He didn't care. What if they merely caught Kane? What if they put him back in the prison system—a prison system that couldn't seem to hold him? What if he got away?

Cord started back in the direction of his car. "Kane's not getting away this time." If he had to put a bullet in the bastard's head right in front of a bunch of cops to make sure, he would accept the consequences.

"Cord, wait."

"Hold your breath, McCaskey."

"A call just came through. There's a man down. On one of the piers right there near the Union."

Cord spun back to the lake. Sure enough, a small crowd gathered on the pier farthest out. He couldn't tell for sure in the dim light, but it appeared they were looking down at something on the pier. Something that could be a man. "Got it."

"Cord—"

He slapped the phone closed and started running. Dodging partying students, he raced around the stage and along the concrete rimming the lakeshore. His boots slammed against the pavement. The sound of his pulse beat in his ears, mixing with reggae. He pushed harder, lengthening his stride, approaching the pier.

Boards shaking beneath his feet with each footfall, he closed the distance to the small crowd. Sirens wailed from a nearby street, screaming over the music.

He kept running. Finally he reached the crowd. "Get out of the way!"

A couple of older-looking people turned to look at him, but they didn't step to the side. A woman darted backward, almost losing her balance and falling in the water.

Cord grabbed her arm to steady her, then bulled his way through. He knelt down beside the body. Even in the dark, he recognized Bryce Walker immediately. "Bryce?" He checked his neck for a pulse. Blood met his hand, warm and sticky. The beat drummed steady against his fingers.

Walker groaned.

He crouched low, until his cheek almost touched the boards. "What happened?"

"I…didn't see him."

A hum rose in Cord's ears. "Kane?"

"He knifed me…he took the boat."

"And the others?"

"On the boat. Oh God, they're all on the boat."

Cord looked out to the water. Behind him, flashing red lights poured over the pier and reflected off the waves. An ambulance drove to the lake's edge.

Cord grasped Bryce's shoulder and lowered his

mouth back to the attorney's ear. "The paramedics are here. They'll take care of you. I'm going after Kane."

Bryce struggled to move his head, to look at him with pain-dull eyes. "Go."

The pier thundered with the approach of running paramedics.

Cord scrambled to his feet. He looked out across the dark water. A light shone in the distance. A light he swore had to be from a large boat.

He tried to breathe, tried to think. The boat was too far out to reach by swimming. Even if he could make it that far, it would take too long. And likely he would be too tired to be of much use once he got there.

He spotted several canoes on the edge of the water. A lanky kid was loading them onto a trailer with other canoes and locking them down. Dodging paramedics wheeling a stretcher to Bryce, he raced for the canoes.

Oblivious to the drama unfolding just yards away on the pier, the kid worked like a drone. He picked up the last canoe and hefted it up to the trailer.

"Wait!"

The kid stopped. He looked up, the expression on his face a mixture of annoyance and disbelief.

Cord leaped off the side of the pier and landed on the concrete next to the kid. "I'll take that canoe."

"Sorry. Too late."

"I need it. This is urgent."

"Like I said, sorry. I'm packing up."

If he had to pull his gun on the kid, he would. "I'm not fooling around." He unsnapped the holster at his side.

"You robbing me?" The kid glared at him. He didn't even look scared. He looked angry, offended.

That was it. Cord didn't need a weapon to handle this. He grabbed the canoe and ripped it from the skinny kid's grasp.

"Hey, you can't do that!"

He threw the canoe in the water and grabbed a paddle from the stack.

"Stop. That ain't yours." The kid lunged at him, grabbing his waist. Stumbling over his own damn feet, he fell to the concrete.

Cord whipped around, giving the kid a *Murder One* stare. He raised the paddle. "Back off."

The kid held up his hands. "Take it easy."

Spinning around, Cord waded down the steps and into the water. He steadied the canoe and stepped in. It tipped and bobbed, but he managed to get in and sit on the seat without tipping over. Thrusting the paddle into the water, he started paddling.

Shouts sounded from behind him. The kid, the paramedics, he didn't know. And he wasn't about to turn around and find out.

He dug the paddle into the water and pulled, stroke after stroke. He had to get to that boat. He had to stop Kane. He had to reach Melanie and Ethan and his sisters before it was too late.

The lake stretched black in front of him, lights rimming the shores. The wind had died down, but the waves still bucked him in the air. He fought back, stroking as hard as he could. He focused on a light out in the water, the one he'd thought was the boat. The one he *prayed* was the boat. His arms began to burn.

All he'd ever wanted was on that boat. All he'd ever needed. Melanie. His son. His sisters, too. *His family.* He wasn't going to let Kane steal them from him.

He'd kill the bastard and cut out his heart first.

After paddling for what seemed like an eternity, he could make out the white outline of the boat. That was it. That was the one.

A muffled scream rose over the lapping of waves.

Anger slammed through him, hot and hard. He wanted Kane dead. He wanted to strangle him and watch his eyes bulge when he died.

Choking back the rage, he locked it inside, ready to use it. To summon it forth when the moment was at hand.

Maybe Kane was right. Maybe Cord was a chip off the old block. Maybe he was a killer at heart. He just hoped his father appreciated the irony. Because right now dear old dad was the one in his sights.

He stroked for all he was worth. Finally reaching the boat, he pulled the canoe alongside and positioned it as close to the ladder as he could.

He stood in the tippy vessel and grabbed the ladder's cold steel. Climbing hand over hand, he forced his tired muscles to pull him up the ladder. Near the top, he reached to his holster for the gun.

The holster was empty.

Damn, damn, damn. Back at the pier. When the kid lunged at him, he'd grabbed hold of his waist to stop him from taking the canoe. He must have knocked the gun out. That or it slipped out later when he was in the canoe.

He looked down at the water. The canoe drifted on the waves, already bobbing fifteen feet from the boat.

The canoe or the shore, either way he was out of luck.

It didn't matter. He didn't have a second to lose, a moment to hesitate. He'd already heard one scream. If he didn't stop Kane now, there would be others. He just prayed he wasn't already too late.

He pulled himself over the rail and into the boat. Red lights from shore pulsed off the deck. No, red *and* blue. Cord glanced back at the Union. Sure enough, cop cars had joined the ambulance. Reed must be on his way.

Too bad he couldn't wait.

He knelt down and slipped off his boots. The last thing he needed to do was thunder around on deck and tip off Kane below. He had to be quiet. Without a weapon of any kind, he had to rely on surprise. It was his only chance.

A weapon.

He remembered the night they'd boarded the boat. Bryce had been behind the wheel. He'd emerged with a rifle.

He started across the deck, moving as quietly as he could. If the rifle was still there, he might have a chance.

He passed the door leading down to the cabins and moved to the front of the boat. Stepping in front of the console, he scanned the area for any place Bryce could have stashed his rifle. Two prongs to the right of the console caught his eye. A gun rack.

An *empty* gun rack.

His pulse pounded in his ears, louder than the waves lapping against the hull. He could only hope Kane didn't have the rifle with him. At the hotel he'd had nothing but a knife. If he'd gotten his hands on a gun since then, this might be a very short rescue.

He stepped from the bridge and headed back toward the steps leading to the hold. A shrill bleat cut through the night.

His cell phone.

He grabbed the thing from his belt. Fingers fumbling, he punched it on, heading off a second ring.

For a moment he just stood perfectly still. If Kane had heard the ring, would he come to investigate? Or would he speed up his killing?

No sound reached him but the lap of waves and the pounding of his own heart. He held the phone to his ear. "Yeah?" he whispered.

"Nikki was in the car," McCaskey said. "In the trunk."

Cord's throat closed. "Dead?"

"No. But she was in pretty bad shape. She says he left her alive so he could hunt her later. And there's another thing."

"What?"

"It was Nikki. She was the leak. She was trying to trap Kane." McCaskey's voice sounded rough with emotion.

Cord could just imagine how betrayed he felt. Cord would like to have a word with Nikki himself. But she would have to wait. "I'm on the boat."

"What?"

"I'm out on Walker's boat. Kane is below."

"I'm on my way."

"I'm not waiting." He closed the phone. In the dark, he couldn't see the button to turn the damn thing off. So not wanting to risk having it ring again, he tossed it over the side and started down the steps.

He was about halfway down when he heard the hum of voices. When he reached the kitchen, Kane's low monotone rose over the sound of the waves. "It's every boy's dream to kill his mother. Isn't it?"

"Leave her alone," Ethan shouted.

Cord's stomach clenched. Kane couldn't be forcing Ethan—

He couldn't even think about it. He had to find a weapon. He had to take Kane out before he could do anymore harm than he already had.

"I always wanted to listen to my mother scream, listen to her beg. To treat her like trash. The way she treated me."

Cord yanked open one kitchen drawer after another. As quietly as he could, he rummaged inside. It was so dark, it was hard to see. But there had to be a knife here. There had to be.

"Get away from her."

"Ethan." Melanie's voice trembled. "It's okay. Please, he'll hurt you."

Cord's hand touched a blade. He pulled a boning knife from the drawer. Grabbing the locked knob, he lowered a shoulder and slammed into the cabin door.

The wood splintered and flew open. He lunged into the room.

Diana, Ethan and Melanie sat tied on the bed. Sylvie lay on the floor.

Reaching across Melanie, Kane held a knife blade in front of Ethan's face. Before he could react to Cord, Melanie threw her body forward, slamming her forehead right above Kane's ear.

Kane swayed. He reached out to the mattress to steady himself. The knife fell from his hand and landed on the mattress between Mel and Ethan.

Melanie rolled toward Ethan, shielding the boy with her body.

Cord lunged across the tiny room. He threw himself on Kane, knocking the killer flat to the mattress. He grabbed Kane's left arm and twisted it behind his back. With his other hand, Cord held the boning knife to the side of the monster's throat.

One slash and he could slice Kane's carotid artery. One flick of the wrist and Dryden Kane would die in minutes. No more threat. No more games. There would finally be justice for all those women. And the men who had gotten in his way.

If Cord wanted, it would all be over. Just like that.

Silence hung in the cabin. No sound except Kane's labored breathing.

He could feel Melanie's eyes focus on him.

He could feel Ethan's eyes.

Kane hadn't taken them. He hadn't stolen them. They would have that future, that bright future Melanie had talked about. A future that might just include him.

Unless he did what he wanted to do. What he was burning to do.

Unless he killed Kane.

He shoved his knee in the small of Kane's back and leaned on him with all his weight. He hadn't let Kane steal his future. And he'd be damned if he'd throw it away this time. Not for any reason.

He would have to trust the system to work. Trust the authorities to keep Kane locked up. Trust the police to keep him and his family safe. Taking a deep breath, he pulled the knife away from the killer's throat.

He looked up, into Melanie's tear-streaked face. Into her beautiful smile. And for the first time in his life, he knew without a doubt he belonged.

Shoving a hand in the killer's pockets, he found a handcuff key. He held it up and turned to Mel. "The sooner you can get those cuffs off Diana, the sooner I can put them on him."

Climbing to her knees, she opened her hands where they were tied behind her back and he dropped the key into one palm. Maneuvering back-to-back with Diana, Mel started working on the cuffs.

Kane grunted under his breath. "You're wasting your talent. Your power."

"Shut up, Kane."

Footfalls sounded from the deck. McCaskey. The police. No doubt McCaskey wouldn't be thrilled Kane was alive, but that was his problem. Cord was no murderer. It wasn't in him. And he knew that whatever happened with Kane, Cord was ready to bask in that bright future. A future with Melanie and Ethan by his side.

"Cord!" Diana screamed. "He has a—"

Mel rolled over Ethan shielding him.

Cord saw the weapon. He saw Kane's hand rise. He saw the barrel level straight at him.

Bam, bam, bam.

Kane's head exploded. His hand fell to the mattress. His body went limp.

Standing in the doorway, Reed McCaskey lowered his weapon.

Epilogue

The minister stood at the front of the old white church with the steeple and talked about love and marriage and all sorts of junk like that.

Well, not junk really. Ethan liked some of the stuff he was saying. The stuff about his mom and dad being together forever, through good times and bad. He figured they'd already gotten a lot of those bad times out of the way. Now he was ready for the good.

Ethan's mom and dad had been planning this wedding for months. Picking out clothes and music and food. They'd even let him eat cake samples and choose the one he liked best. And the day of their wedding had finally arrived.

Ethan looked up at his parents. Mom *and* Dad. He liked the sound. He liked that they were all living together in his house. He liked just about everything. The good times had already begun.

Even the counselor he'd been seeing wasn't too bad. She was so nice he didn't even feel bad about telling her all that had happened. Finding his dad. And all that stuff with his grandfather, Dryden Kane.

He didn't think about Kane as much anymore. For a while after what had happened in Uncle Bryce's boat, he'd had nightmares. He'd wake up screaming, the sound of gunfire still ringing in his ears. But his nightmares were gone now. He could even concentrate on school again. And even though he had to go to summer school so he could pass into sixth grade, he'd deal.

A squeal echoed through the little white church. Ethan looked back at the pews. Uncle Bryce and Aunt Sylvie sat in the first row, his baby cousin, Ronnie, in Aunt Sylvie's lap. If you asked him, Ronnie looked ridiculous in her frilly little dress and that lacy band around her head. Like some kind of commercial for dumb girly baby stuff. But no one asked him, so he didn't say anything.

For Christmas, he'd give her a Brett Favre jersey. After all, that's what cousins were for.

Pleased with the idea, he grinned up at Aunt Diana, who stood beside Mom. Aunt Diana was going to have a baby, too. Her tummy looked so big in her matron-of-honor dress, he was betting she'd have two. He sure hoped they would be boys. He'd be really outnumbered if he had three girl cousins.

Heck if he did, he'd buy them all Packer jerseys and teach them how to wrestle.

Uncle Reed stood up at the front of the church with them. He was wearing a tuxedo, just like Dad and Ethan, only Uncle Reed looked like James Bond in his. Ethan wondered if he had his gun, or maybe the gun was hidden in the heel of one of those shiny shoes.

"The rings?"

Even if Uncle Reed was like James Bond, no one was as cool as Dad.

"Ahem."

All the times he'd wanted a dad, he'd imagined a lot of things. How strong his dad would be, how smart, how he would help Ethan and his mom and laugh with them and do cool stuff with them. But having Cord for his dad was more than he'd ever imagined. And someday Ethan wanted to grow up to be just as strong and smart as he was.

"Ethan?" Dad's whispered voice cut through his thoughts.

He looked up. "Yeah?"

Dad held out his hand. "The rings. You got 'em?"

Quiet hung in the church, and Ethan suddenly realized everybody was looking at him. His cheeks got hot.

Mom smiled. "In your pocket."

He reached into his pocket. His fingers touched nothing but a piece of lint.

He looked at Mom then Dad, his heart beating so loud the whole church must hear.

Dad put a steady hand on Ethan's shoulder. "Your other pocket."

Ethan shoved his hand into the other one. He touched metal bands. Smiling, he pulled them out and gave them to Dad.

That was close.

Dad gave one to Mom and they slipped them on each other's fingers. Then together they said the words Ethan had heard them both practicing for at least the last month. "I take you to be my partner in life and my one true love. I will trust you and respect you, laugh with you and cry with you, loving you faithfully through good times and bad, regardless of the obstacles we may face together. I give you my hand, my heart and my love, from this day forward for as long as we both shall live."

Ethan blinked his eyes and brushed his cheeks with the back of one hand. So it was a little mushy. So what?

The next book in
THE BRIDES OF BELLA LUCIA *series*
is out next month!
Don't miss THE REBEL PRINCE
by Raye Morgan
Here's an exclusive sneak preview
of Emma Valentine's story!

"OH, NO!"

The reaction slipped out before Emma Valentine could stop it, for there stood the very man she most wanted to avoid seeing again.

He didn't look any happier to see her.

"Well, come on, get on board," he said gruffly. "I won't bite." One eyebrow rose. "Though I might nibble a little," he added, mostly to amuse himself.

But she wasn't paying any attention to what he was saying. She was staring at him, taking in the royal blue uniform he was wearing, with gold braid and glistening badges decorating the sleeves, epaulettes and an upright collar. Ribbons and medals covered the breast of the short, fitted jacket. A gold-encrusted sabre hung at his side. And suddenly it was clear to her who this man really was.

She gulped wordlessly. Reaching out, he took

her elbow and pulled her aboard. The doors slid closed. And finally she found her tongue.

"You…you're the prince."

He nodded, barely glancing at her. "Yes. Of course."

She raised a hand and covered her mouth for a moment. "I should have known."

"Of course you should have. I don't know why you didn't." He punched the ground-floor button to get the elevator moving again, then turned to look down at her. "A relatively bright five-year-old child would have tumbled to the truth right away."

Her shock faded as her indignation at his tone asserted itself. He might be the prince, but he was still just as annoying as he had been earlier that day.

"A relatively bright five-year-old child without a bump on the head from a badly thrown water polo ball, maybe," she said defensively. She wasn't feeling woozy any longer and she wasn't about to let him bully her, no matter how royal he was. "I was unconscious half the time."

"And just clueless the other half, I guess," he said, looking bemused.

The arrogance of the man was really galling.

"I suppose you think your 'royalness' is so obvious it sort of shimmers around you for all to see?" she challenged. "Or better yet, oozes from your pores like…like sweat on a hot day?"

"Something like that," he acknowledged calmly. "Most people tumble to it pretty quickly. In fact, it's hard to hide even when I want to avoid dealing with it."

"Poor baby," she said, still resenting his manner. "I guess that works better with injured people who are half asleep." Looking at him, she felt a strange emotion she couldn't identify. It was as though she wanted to prove something to him, but she wasn't sure what. "And anyway, you know you did your best to fool me," she added.

His brows knit together as though he really didn't know what she was talking about. "I didn't do a thing."

"You told me your name was Monty."

"It is." He shrugged. "I have a lot of names. Some of them are too rude to be spoken to my face, I'm sure." He glanced at her sideways, his hand on the hilt of his sabre. "Perhaps you're contemplating one of those right now."

You bet I am.

That was what she would like to say. But it suddenly occurred to her that she was supposed to be working for this man. If she wanted to keep the job of coronation chef, maybe she'd better keep her opinions to herself. So she clamped her mouth shut, took a deep breath and looked away, trying hard to calm down.

The elevator ground to a halt and the doors slid open laboriously. She moved to step forward, hoping to make her escape, but his hand shot out again and caught her elbow.

"Wait a minute. *You're* a woman," he said, as though that thought had just presented itself to him.

"That's a rare ability for insight you have there, Your Highness," she snapped before she could stop herself. And then she winced. She was going to have to do better than that if she was going to keep this relationship on an even keel.

But he was ignoring her dig. Nodding, he stared at her with a speculative gleam in his golden eyes. "I've been looking for a woman, but you'll do."

She blanched, stiffening. "I'll do for what?"

He made a head gesture in a direction she knew was opposite of where she was going and his grip tightened on her elbow.

"Come with me," he said abruptly, making it an order.

She dug in her heels, thinking fast. She didn't much like orders. "Wait! I can't. I have to get to the kitchen."

"Not yet. I need you."

"You what?" Her breathless gasp of surprise was soft, but she knew he'd heard it.

"I need you," he said firmly. "Oh, don't look so shocked. I'm not planning to throw you into the hay and have my way with you. I need you for something a bit more mundane than that."

She felt color rushing into her cheeks and she silently begged it to stop. Here she was, formless and stodgy in her chef's whites. No makeup, no stiletto heels. Hardly the picture of the femmes fatales he was undoubtedly used to. The likelihood that he would have any carnal interest in her was remote at best. To have him think she was hysterically defending her virtue was humiliating.

"Well, what if I don't want to go with you?" she said in hopes of deflecting his attention from her blush.

"Too bad."

"What?"

Amusement sparkled in his eyes. He was certainly enjoying this. And that only made her more determined to resist him.

"I'm the prince, remember? And we're in the castle. My orders take precedence. It's that old pesky divine rights thing."

Her jaw jutted out. Despite her embarrassment, she couldn't let that pass.

"Over my free will? Never!"

Exasperation filled his face.

"Hey, call out the historians. Someone will write a book about you and your courageous principles." His eyes glittered sardonically. "But in the meantime, Emma Valentine, you're coming with me."

HARLEQUIN *Romance*

The family saga continues…

The Brides of Bella Lucia

THE REBEL PRINCE by Raye Morgan

Just an ordinary girl and…a jet-setting playboy of a prince who is about to be crowned king!

Prince Sebastian has one last act of rebellion in store, and it involves giving chef Emma Valentine a brand-new title!

ON SALE SEPTEMBER 2006.

From the Heart. For the Heart.

www.eHarlequin.com

HRIBC0806BW

SAVE UP TO $30! SIGN UP TODAY!

INSIDE *Romance*

The complete guide to your favorite
Harlequin®, Silhouette® and Love Inspired® books.

✓ Newsletter ABSOLUTELY FREE! No purchase necessary.

✓ Valuable coupons for future purchases of Harlequin,
Silhouette and Love Inspired books in every issue!

✓ Special excerpts & previews in each issue. Learn about all
the hottest titles before they arrive in stores.

✓ No hassle—mailed directly to your door!

✓ Comes complete with a handy shopping checklist
so you won't miss out on any titles.

- -

SIGN ME UP TO RECEIVE INSIDE ROMANCE
ABSOLUTELY FREE

(Please print clearly)

_____

Name

_____

Address

_____

City/Town   State/Province   Zip/Postal Code

(098 KKM EJL9)

Please mail this form to:
In the U.S.A.: Inside Romance, P.O. Box 9057, Buffalo, NY 14269-9057
In Canada: Inside Romance, P.O. Box 622, Fort Erie, ON L2A 5X3
OR visit http://www.eHarlequin.com/insideromance

IRNBPA06R   ® and ™ are trademarks owned and used by the trademark owner and/or its licensee.

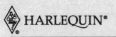

HARLEQUIN®

American ROMANCE®

IS PROUD TO PRESENT A
GUEST APPEARANCE BY

QUILL
BOOK
AWARD
WINNING
AUTHOR

NEW YORK TIMES bestselling author
DEBBIE MACOMBER

The Wyoming Kid

The story of an ex–rodeo cowboy,
a schoolteacher and their journey to the altar.

"Best-selling Macomber, with more than
100 romances and women's fiction titles
to her credit, sure has a way of pleasing readers."
—*Booklist* on *Between Friends*

***The Wyoming Kid* is available from
Harlequin American Romance in July 2006.**

www.eHarlequin.com   HARDMJUL

**Introducing an exciting appearance
by legendary
New York Times bestselling author**

DIANA PALMER

HEARTBREAKER

He's the ultimate bachelor...
but he may have just met
the one woman to change his ways!

Join the drama in the story of a confirmed
bachelor, an amnesiac beauty and their
unexpected passionate romance.

**"Diana Palmer is a mesmerizing storyteller
who captures the essence of what
a romance should be."** *—Affaire de Coeur*

**Heartbreaker *is available from Silhouette Desire
in September 2006.***

Visit Silhouette Books at www.eHarlequin.com   SDDPIBC

HARLEQUIN

Blaze

"Super-steamy!"
—*Cosmopolitan* magazine

New York Times bestselling author

Elizabeth Bevarly

delivers another sexy adventure!

As a former vice cop, small-town police chief
Sam Maguire knows when things don't add up.
And there's definitely something suspicious happen-
ing behind the scenes at Rosie Bliss's flower shop.
Rumor has it she's not selling just flowers.
But once he gets close and gets his hands on her,
uh, goods, he's in big trouble…of the sensual kind!

Pick up your copy of

MY ONLY VICE

by Elizabeth Bevarly

*Available this September,
wherever series romances are sold.*

www.eHarlequin.com   HBEB0906

ANGELS OF THE BIG SKY
by Roz Denny Fox

(#1368)

Widow Marlee Stein returns to Montana with her
young daughter, ready to help out with Cloud Chasers,
the flying service owned by her brother. When Marlee
takes over piloting duties, she finds herself in conflict
with a client, ranger Wylie Ames. Too bad Marlee's
attracted to a man she doesn't even want to like!

On sale September 2006!

THE CLOUD CHASERS—
Life is looking up.

Watch for the second story in Roz Denny Fox's two-
book series THE CLOUD CHASERS, available in
December 2006.

*Available wherever books are sold, including most
bookstores, supermarkets, discount stores and drugstores.*

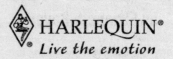

If you enjoyed what you just read,
then we've got an offer you can't resist!

Take 2 bestselling love stories FREE!

Plus get a FREE surprise gift!

Clip this page and mail it to Harlequin Reader Service®

IN U.S.A.
3010 Walden Ave.
P.O. Box 1867
Buffalo, N.Y. 14240-1867

IN CANADA
P.O. Box 609
Fort Erie, Ontario
L2A 5X3

YES! Please send me 2 free Harlequin Intrigue® novels and my free surprise gift. After receiving them, if I don't wish to receive anymore, I can return the shipping statement marked cancel. If I don't cancel, I will receive 4 brand-new novels each month, before they're available in stores! In the U.S.A., bill me at the bargain price of $4.24 plus 25¢ shipping and handling per book and applicable sales tax, if any*. In Canada, bill me at the bargain price of $4.99 plus 25¢ shipping and handling per book and applicable taxes**. That's the complete price and a savings of at least 10% off the cover prices—what a great deal! I understand that accepting the 2 free books and gift places me under no obligation ever to buy any books. I can always return a shipment and cancel at any time. Even if I never buy another book from Harlequin, the 2 free books and gift are mine to keep forever.

181 HDN DZ7N
381 HDN DZ7P

Name _____ (PLEASE PRINT)

Address _____ Apt.#

City _____ State/Prov. _____ Zip/Postal Code

Not valid to current Harlequin Intrigue® subscribers.

Want to try two free books from another series?
Call 1-800-873-8635 or visit www.morefreebooks.com.

* Terms and prices subject to change without notice. Sales tax applicable in N.Y.
** Canadian residents will be charged applicable provincial taxes and GST.
All orders subject to approval. Offer limited to one per household.
® are registered trademarks owned and used by the trademark owner and or its licensee.

INT04R   ©2004 Harlequin Enterprises Limited

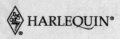

INTRIGUE®

COMING NEXT MONTH

#939 LOOK-ALIKE by Rita Herron
Nighthawk Island
Sheriff Miles Monahue is looking for the love of his life. Instead, he finds two of her, one dead and an identical twin with no memory.

#940 OPERATION: MIDNIGHT RENDEZVOUS
by Linda Castillo
After Jessica Atwood rescues her best friend's child one terrifying night, it'll take the strength and cunning of agent Mike Madrid to uncover Lighthouse Point's unsettling secrets.

#941 WITHOUT A DOUBT by Kathleen Long
Years ago, a house fire changed television reporter Sophie Markham's life forever. But when an assignment has her cross paths with former flame Gary Barksdale and a very special little girl, her life may change all over again.

#942 A CLANDESTINE AFFAIR by Joanna Wayne
Cape Diablo
Ravaged by passion, Jaci Matlock and Raoul Lazario will need to learn how to trust each other if they're to survive an age-old murderous conspiracy.

#943 ON FIRE by Jan Hambright
As children, fire investigator Kade Decker and psychologist Savannah Dawson were joined by a psychic connection. Now, that bond brings them back together again when their town falls under the grip of an arsonist.

#944 SILENT MEMORIES by Pat White
Scientist Annie Price is going to need FBI agent Sean MacNeil's determination to stop her research from being used to hold the world hostage, but can she first save him from the violent demons that haunt him?

www.eHarlequin.com

HICNM0806